Spud Sweetgrass

Also by Brian Doyle

Angel Square
Covered Bridge
Easy Avenue
Hey, Dad!
Up to Low
You Can Pick Me Up at Peggy's Cove

Brian Doyle

Spud
Sweetgrass

A Groundwood Book
Douglas & McIntyre
TORONTO / VANCOUVER / BUFFALO

Special thanks to: Wilf Pelletier, who knows how to make it rain by dancing; Jim Dillon, who knows how propane tanks blow; Marlene Stanton, for helping research Bank Street; Mike Paradis, for the invaluable critique; Jacques Dussault, for the use of Westboro Beach, Sue Wong, for the help with the names; the Kocoris and Langis boys at the Easy Street Café, for explaining cooking oil; and the humble potato.

The author gratefully acknowledges permission from *Clark Parry Doyle Productions* to reproduce the song "Fry-Day" from the musical, "Chipwagon!" © 1982.

Groundwood Books/Douglas & McIntyre Ltd.
585 Bloor Street West
Toronto, Ontario M6G 1K5

The publisher gratefully acknowledges the assistance of the Ontario Arts Council and the Canada Council.

Canadian Cataloguing in Publication Data

Doyle, Brian
    Spud Sweetgrass

ISBN 0-88899-189-4

I. Title.

PS8557.087S6   1993   jC813'.54   C93-094332-5
PZ7.D79Sp   1993

Design by Michael Solomon
Cover art by Paul Zwolak
Printed and bound in Canada

This book is dedicated
to my grandson
Matthew Patrick Doyle

❧
―――――

Prologue

I walked with my mother and my father into the bush. My father was carrying his trombone in its case.

In about an hour we came to the shore of a small lake.

It was my birthday. I was nine.

Beside the lake, my father took out of his trombone case three things: a knife; a fishing line with a hook; one wooden match.

"You will stay here by yourself until after breakfast tomorrow morning," he said. My mother stood beside him and took his arm.

"You will cut balsam boughs to make a shelter for yourself. You will build a fire and be sure that it doesn't go out during the night. You will catch a fish for your supper and another one for your breakfast. There are berries and butternuts and wild garlic around to eat, too.

"We will be ten minutes from here. But you will not know which way. You will not be able to find us."

I was watching my mother. She had a nice look on her face. Her brown eyes were proud of me.

They were holding me. There were green flecks flashing.

"But you can call to us if you are in trouble. You call by blowing a long strong note on my trombone. But only take it out of the case if there's an emergency," my father said.

My mother had a small smile on her beautiful face. Her head was tilted to one side. There was love all around the shore of that small lake.

"You will be alone," said my father, "this afternoon, this evening and all night, which will be the hardest part."

My mother's smile got bigger.

"We will be back to get you after breakfast," she said. Then they both put their arms around me.

And then they kissed me.

And then they walked into the bush and disappeared.

I

I don't like Dumper Stubbs.

I don't know if it's the way he looks or the way he acts or the clothes he wears, or what, I just don't like him.

My mother always used to say that you should get to know people before you figure out if you like them or you don't like them. Then she and my father would start talking about exceptions. "But every rule has some exceptions," my father would start. Then they'd have this funny conversation.

"Of course," my father would say, "people with very large chins are basically very cruel people. And people with their eyes very close together are very stupid . . ." And then my mother would say, ". . . and people with very large heads can't control themselves and people with big, low ears are gossips." And then my father might say, while he started to laugh, "and people whose nostrils flare out are perverts and people who walk with their toes pointing outwards never wash themselves properly." And then they'd both be laughing and saying stuff like people who walked with their hands in their pockets were thieves and people who slouched were cowards, and people with loud voices were bullies and people with bad breath were liars and women who smoked were two-faced and men who wore their pants high were abusers and they'd keep on like that until they couldn't think of any more and then they'd say, both together, "but you can't judge a book by its *cover!*"

And they would laugh all over again and then go across the street to the Village Inn to see their friends.

My mother and father don't do that stuff together anymore.

My father died last September of a brain tumour.

And my mother, I don't know what's wrong with her. She seems different now.

So, here comes Dumper Stubbs to pick up the garbage and change the grease.

And I don't like him.

Dumper has a large chin, close-together eyes, a big head, low ears, flared nostrils, pointed-out toes, his hands in his pockets, a slouch, a loud voice, bad breath and high pants.

And I miss my father, who was big and handsome and brave.

Oh, if only now I could blow a long note on his trombone and he'd be only ten minutes away!

Maybe that's why I hate Dumper.

Because he's alive. He's alive and my father is dead. It just isn't fair.

And also, I hate him because he called my father a name.

"Is your father that stupid Abo that used to play that funny-looking horn over at that stupid club?" he said once.

Dumper Stubbs is going to pay for that.

II

C all me Spud.

My real name is John. John Sweetgrass. But everybody calls me Spud. They started calling me that when I got hired to work in the chipwagon. I'm part Irish and part Abo and part of a whole lot of other things. Abo is short for Aboriginal. My girlfriend (she's not really my girlfriend, I just call her that) is half Vietnamese and half Chinese. Her name is Connie Pan.

The first time I ever talked to Connie Pan was at Ottawa Tech the day I chased the guys away from the Muslim on his rug. There was a student who was a Muslim praying on his little rug in the corner of the hallway and there was a bunch of smart asses bugging him. I chased them away. Connie Pan came up and talked to me right after that.

If I married Connie Pan and we had babies, the babies would be part Chinese, part Vietnamese, part Irish, part Abo and part of a whole lot of other things. What a mix-up! I wonder what they'd look like. Probably they'd be very beautiful and handsome and sized average. The reason I think that is that Connie pan is very beautiful and quite tiny and I'm quite handsome and very large.

But that will probably never happen because Connie Pan's mother doesn't want her to hang around with me. Specially since I got kicked out of school. She didn't like me before I got kicked out of school and now she doesn't like me even worse. Her mother calls me "Bignose." Connie Pan says she calls all Canadians Bignose.

Like I said, I work in a chipwagon.

The inside of a chipwagon is hot. Inside of a chipwagon, on the hottest day of July in Ottawa, is very hot. The inside of a chipwagon, in July, on the hottest day of the year in Ottawa, on Somerset Street, in Chinatown, at 1:00 in the afternoon is . . .

My friend Dink the Thinker who looks like a fox and who is always thinking, says it's hotter than Death Valley, California, which is the second hottest place on earth. Dink looked it up. Dink looks everything up. The hottest place on earth is El Azizia, in Libya.

"Could even be hotter than El Azizia," says Dink the Thinker, "which is in the country of Libya. Libya is part of the continent of Africa which is . . ."

"I know where Libya is, Dink," I say. "You don't have to tell me where Libya is. I'm not deep fried yet, you know. Maybe my brain is approaching the boiling point of vegetable oil I admit. So would yours be if you were standing in here up to your neck in sizzling grease, but I'm not fried yet. I still know stuff. I know where Libya is. It's in Africa."

"That's what I said," says Dink.

"And I know where I am," I say. "I'm in a chipwagon on Somerset Street in Chinatown in Ottawa in July. And it's HOT!"

A customer steps up. A guy from my school. (What used to be my school.)

Dink the Thinker moves out of the way.

"What sizes have you got?" says the customer. I recognize him. He was here yesterday. And the day before. He asked the same thing yesterday. And the day before. The sample containers are pinned on the board right in front of his face. On each cardboard container I have printed the size and the price in magic marker.

They are so obvious that it's embarrassing. I think maybe he's kidding. I look closer at his face, into his eyes. No, he's not kidding. His eyes tell me that he's serious. I decide I'm going to put flashing Christmas tree lights on these empty boxes and hook up a little ambulance siren that I can press when this customer comes along again. Breep! Breep! Breep!

With one finger pointing at the display, with my eyes right in his, I tell him: "Small, medium, large, jumbo and family."

He looks up at the display.

I wait.

Suddenly, I know what he's going to do. He's going to ask how much they are! The prices are written right on the boxes in big block letters in red magic marker. He's looking right at the display. He reads each box.

Then his eyes come slowly back to mine. Then he says it.

"How much are they?"

"Depends on what size you want," I say, looking over at Dink.

"El Azizia is in Libya," Dink says.

"How big is the small one?" my customer says.

"Smaller than the medium one," I say, catching with my tongue a silver bead of salty sweat that's been dangling from my nose.

"Got any hot dogs?" my customer asks.

That's it. Death Valley. El Azizia. Somerset Street. What's the difference? It's hot. Do I care if I make this sale? No! Would my boss care if he were here? Who cares?

"Look on the truck here," I say. "It says *Beethoven's Classical Chips*. Right? Then, on the front of the truck, look at it, it will say, French Fries, then on the back of the truck — Beethoven's Chips; then on the other side of the truck — Beethoven's Chips; then in smaller print it says Fries, cold drinks. Then there's a sign that says 'Come in, We're open.' Now, do you see 'hot dogs' written anywhere on this truck? Take a look around. Do you even see a picture of a hot dog anywhere around here? Look on this counter. Do you see any mustard here? Relish? Ketchup? No. What do you see? You see vinegar, you see salt, you see toothpicks, you see serviettes. Now, start figuring it out . . ."

"I'll have a small fries," says my customer, now that he's got it all straightened out in his head.

"Sold!" I cry, and I lower the basket cage into the boiling oil. There is a crash of bubbling and popping and in a cloud of greasy steam I disappear for a minute.

I can hear Dink talking to my customer. "Do you know that it's hotter here today on Somerset Street than it is in Libya, which is in Africa?"

"What do you mean?" says my customer.

Then I hear Dink saying, louder than normal, so I'll hear him, "Good afternoon Mr. Fryday! Lovely day!"

Mr. Fryday! My boss. Owner of a chain, a string, a fleet of famous chipwagons around Ottawa and Hull. Beethoven's Classical Chips. Mozart's Chips. Tchaikovsky's Chips. Handel's Chips. Rimsky-Korsakov's Chips. Holtz's Chips . . . get it? I hit my player button and the Beethoven, somewhere in the middle of the first movement of Symphony No. 7, comes charging out of the speakers.

I stick my head out of the fog with my customer's cardboard container half filled.

"Salt and vinegar in the middle, sir?" I say, hosing politeness all over my customer, my owner, my friend Dink and up and down the sidewalk and into the Mekong Grocery.

"What do you mean?" says the customer, who must have had his brain removed when he was young. I decide that when Dink goes back to school he can find out this guy's name and look up the files, maybe he died at birth.

"Well sir," I say, the politeness and understanding coming out of me is making me feel a little sick, "you see sir, some of our customers like to apply a dash or two of salt in the middle of their order, and sometimes even a shot or two of vinegar so that when we fill in the rest of the order, and then add salt and vinegar to the top, the chips are uniformly salted and vinegared throughout."

Dink, who's always correcting people, says, "Vinegared? No such word."

My boss is getting rich with this great idea of naming his chipwagons after famous composers and having the famous composers' music playing while the chips are selling like hot cakes. I say "selling like hot cakes," because that's what he always says. About his other wagons. Not about the one I run for him. "Tchaikovsky's are selling like hot cakes," he'll say to me one day, "what's wrong with Beethoven's?" Another day he'll say, "Rimsky-Korsakov's Chips are selling like hot cakes, what's wrong with Beethoven's?"

Sometimes I feel like saying, "I have a suggestion, Mr. Fryday. Why don't we switch to selling hot cakes then if they're such a fast moving item?" but I don't say that because I need this job. And anyway, I have to watch my mouth. I'm too mouthy sometimes.

Dink thinks that Mr. Fryday probably tells each of the other chipwagon guys the same line. He probably says to the guy running Mozart's, "Beethoven's Chips are selling like hot cakes. What's wrong with Mozart's?"

I'm going to send Dink around to the other wagons one of these days to find out.

Today Mr. Fryday does his usual taste test, picking one fry out of the tray that I hand out to him, picking one fry up daintily with his chubby thumb and forefinger, the other three fingers sparkling with rings, and delicately tasting his famous fry.

"Could be left in just a few seconds longer," he says, smacking his lips together to help him taste. Darts of sunlight shoot out of his mouth from his gold tooth.

He usually says either that or sometime's he'll say, "You left it in just a couple of seconds too long."

Then he comes out with his usual skill-testing question: "I'm thinking about expanding, selling hot dogs from the wagons. What do you think of that idea from a business point of view, Spud Sweetgrass?"

I give him the usual answer. The one he wants to hear.

"Well sir, it seems to me that adding another product would complicate the production end and also take away from your strong image as the best chipman in Eastern Ontario, or perhaps, Ontario. I don't think it's a good idea."

"Excellent! You'll go places as an entrepreneur my boy! Carry on!"

He leaves, swinging his silver-handled walking stick, just as the last part of the First Movement of Beethoven's Seventh Symphony blasts out across the sidewalk and into the door of the Mekong Grocery Store, shaking the noodles on the shelves.

I don't have to tell you how Mr. Fryday walks. Just listen to the last minute or so of the First Movement of Beethoven's Seventh Symphony.

Then you'll know.

I give Dink the Thinker a loonie to feed the meter. Dink feeds the meter; then takes a picture of Mr. Fryday walking up Somerset Street. Dink takes the picture with an invisible camera. Dink is saving up his money to buy what he's always wanted. A Polaroid camera. For now, since he hasn't quite got enough money saved yet, Dink practises without the camera.

III

I figure Mr. Fryday must have heard me mouthing off at that customer but I wonder why he
didn't say anything to me. Why didn't he say,
"That mouth of yours, that mouth of yours is going
to be your downfall one of these days," like he said
to me the last time he heard me getting sarcastic the
way I do sometimes. When they don't say anything
to you but they give you that look, that's when you
should start to worry.

I know that look.

It's the look the teacher gives when he's decided
to stop giving you any more breaks and starts on
the campaign to turn you in to the man downstairs.
That's what we all called the vice principal of
Ottawa Tech: the man downstairs. Actually there
were three vice principals down there!

I say there *were* three of them down there
because I'm not going back.

I got tossed out right at the end of this year. I
guess I should say there *are* three vice principals
over there. But since I'm not going to be there this
fall, let's say there *were* three vice principals over
there. Because if I'm not there, they don't exist,

right? I'll have to ask Dink about that. That's a deep thought, the kind of deep thought Dink loves. Dink wants to think deep and hard about everything. Dink the Thinker. Dink's ambition when he grows up is to be a contestant on "Jeopardy!" That's why, over at Tech, whenever Dink comes down the hall or comes in the room everybody starts whistling or singing the Jeopardy! song. All of a sudden everybody will stop whatever they're doing and start going "Dee dee dee dee, dee dee dee," etc., singing the words to the Jeopardy! song. Of course, everybody in North America knows the words to the Jeopardy! song. The words are "dee dee dee dee," etc.

Anyway, it drives the teachers crazy. Everytime Dink goes to answer a question or gets out of his desk to get a book or something, we all start "dee dee dee dee," etc. Actually I probably should say, it *drove* everybody crazy because I won't be there for it this fall because I'm not going back.

And if I'm not there, it's not happening. Right?

Let them whistle and sing "dee dee dee dee," etc., without me.

People think you get kicked out of school for *one* thing. Well, you do, sort of, but it's also a kind of build-up.

It starts with "the look."

When they give you "the look," you know things are going to start to happen to you.

We had this new guy come to teach at Tech at the beginning of the second semester in February. He was supposed to be some hotshot English teacher who was going to open up our minds with some kind of a magic can opener or something and change our lives forever.

Right away we started off "on the wrong foot." I think it was because I wouldn't say "have a nice day" to him when the class was over. We had him first period in the morning, from ten after nine to twenty-five after ten. At the end of the class all the sucks from Hong Kong and Cambodia and Viet Nam and Somalia and Bangladesh and Ottawa would all say "have a nice day, sir" on the way by his desk whether they meant it or not. I wonder if, way back in evolution, students in school were related to sheep. I must ask Dink about that

Honest to God, I think that if the first couple of students walked by Boyle's desk and said "have a nice day" and then walked right off a cliff into an abyss of boiling oil, the rest of the students behind them would do the same thing.

I sat at the back, near the windows so I could see the sky during class. I was usually last to get out of the room when the period was over. After all the goodbyes and the bowing and scraping and the have-a-nice-daying. I really stuck out like a sore thumb when I walked by and didn't even look at him.

I would walk by and not even look at him. I think a teacher who hates you because you won't look at him should be fired.

I could often smell him though.

He smelt like stale beer.

For about a month he was really nice to me, always looking right at me when he was explaining stuff or always coming back to my seat to see if he could help me with my work or handing me these great marks which I didn't deserve.

It was the day we all did the Jeopardy! business because Dink walked in late right in the middle of one of Boyle's readings. (He read to us every day in this big deep voice he was really proud of. And he didn't like it unless you were looking really fascinated by his performance. Spellbinding!)

So in walks Dink and I start the Jeopardy! song and everybody joins in and it's really funny and everybody's laughing. Everybody but Boyle. Boyle's bald head is red as a boiled lobster and his beer gut heaving in and out. Suddenly everybody gets it and shuts up.

From then on, I'm getting "the look." It's kind of a blank stare, not friendly, not made, not anything.

Then my marks start going down.

For about two weeks, my marks gradually get lower and every day his eyes follow me out of the room with "the look." Then one day he stops me as I'm leaving the class behind the line of sheep going by his desk and asks me if I thought we were starting off "on the wrong foot."

"What's that mean?" I say to him.

See what I mean, how your mouth can get you in a whole lot of trouble? He knows that I know what that means. And he knows that I *know* that he knows that I know what it means!

"It comes," he says, very quietly, calm in his voice, eyes right in mine, face almost blank, "originally from a military context. Marching, to be specific. You see, you are not marching along with the rest of us. Left, right, left, right. You are marching to some other beat, a different rhythm, a different drummer for some reason. Off on the wrong foot."

"I thought you said 'we,'" I say to him.

"We?" he says.

"Yeah," I say. "You thought *we* were starting off on the wrong foot."

"I meant you."

"But you said, 'we.'"

"Now I'm saying, 'you'!"

We stare at each other for a long time. Boyle wins the staring match. It's almost impossible to outstare a teacher. They must study staring at teachers' training school or somewhere. Boyle probably got an A in staring.

People start coming in for the next class.

I leave.

We are enemies now.

For the whole semester we have a kind of a truce. I don't look at him, he doesn't look at me. My marks stay around the same. Then, just before exams start, I get suspended. Here's how.

I'm standing in the hall talking to my favourite girlfriend, Connie Pan, at lunch time. Along comes Boyle on hall duty.

I'm leaning on the wall with my hands in my pockets. I'm having a real nice time with Connie Pan. We're talking about what kind of presents boys give to girls in her country. It's pretty obvious I'm hinting at maybe I'll give her a present. I tell her that in Canada, if a boy maybe likes a girl, he might, say, just maybe, give her, let's say, just for example, a flower, maybe. A rose maybe. Then she's asking me in this pretty accent what, maybe, present a girl gives a boy in Canada?

I'm leaning on the wall and I've got one knee bent and my foot flat against the wall behind me. I never stand this way. Why am I standing this way? Maybe because I'm talking to Connie Pan. Then I do something else that I never do. I smile at Boyle

22

as he's coming down the hall on lunch hour hall duty. Why am I smiling at Boyle? Who knows. I do crazy things when I'm around girls. Specially girls like Connie Pan.

Suddenly Boyle is right in my face. He looks like he's got a hangover. He smells like cigarettes and beer.

It's like on "Jeopardy!" The answers are away back there, tiny, on the board. Suddenly, one of them is filling the whole screen. Right in your face.

And just like on "Jeopardy!", he gives me the answer first.

"You do this at home all the time."

Then, I give him the question.

"Do what at home?"

"Stand there with your feet all over the walls."

I take my foot down.

"Do you do that at home?" he asks.

I look at Connie Pan. She's looking at the floor. Her little black ponytail is sticking straight back. She looks so delicate and pretty compared to Boyle. Like a flower beside a rhinoceros.

"Do you do that at home?" he repeats.

Suddenly I'm full of hate. I want to smash Boyle's face. I want to kill him. He's putting me down in front of Connie Pan. My father would never do a thing like that. I feel like I felt when I was lighting my one and only wooden match way back when I was nine.

There is no getting out of it. You have to go ahead and light it.

"All the time," I say.

"Let's try this again," he says. "Do you put your feet on the walls at home?"

"Regularly," I say.

"Let's go down and see the man downstairs," he says, and puts his hand out and grabs my arm.

I throw his hand off. I'm just as tall as Boyle. Our noses are almost touching. We look like that famous photograph of the soldier and the Mohawk Warrior that was in all the newspapers during the Oka crisis!

Then I say the two magic words that get you suspended from school every time.

One of them is a word that is used in every language on earth by everybody, according to Dink the Thinker.

The other word is "you."

IV

Today's the day I go to Westboro Beach with Connie Pan. I'm really only *sort of* with Connie Pan, because there's going to be about twenty other people going too. Connie Pan has a part-time job organizing E.S.L. kids from Ottawa Tech to do stuff in the summer. E.S.L. stands for English as a second language. It's a job but she doesn't get paid. She dreams up things to do for the new kids from other countries and then she tries to get kids from Canada to go too. Last week she took them all bowling. The week before they went to the War Museum. Today she's taking them to Westboro Beach.

The hard part about her job is getting the Canadian kids to go, too.

The time she took them up to Champlain's Statue, I was the only Canadian kid there.

Dink the Thinker says that the only reason I go is to be around where Connie Pan is.

As usual, Dink the Thinker is right.

Mr. Fryday will relieve me early today because it's Sunday, and Chinatown is really busy on Sunday, and Mr. Fryday likes to work in his wagon and say hello to everybody and give free orders of chips to his buddies, especially the people who own the shops near where he always parks our wagon.

I'm in a pretty good mood, thinking about going to Westboro Beach, meeting Connie Pan there, having a few cool swims, helping them get organized to play E.S.L. volleyball, without a net, on the sand there.

But, all of a sudden, I'm not in a pretty good mood anymore because here comes Dumper Stubbs, double parking his filthy truck with the big steel bumper beside my nice clean wagon. Dumper's going to empty my trash can, and change my grease. He empties the trash every day. He changes the grease every Sunday.

My wagon has two fryers. One of the fryers is for blanching the chips, the other is for cooking. Mr. Fryday changes the grease once a week in all of his wagons. That's one of the reasons his chips are so good. The other reason is that he doesn't use new potatoes. He uses old potatoes. New potatoes won't get brown in the cooking fryer for some reason. Then, the customers look at them as if there's something wrong with them, they're too white, then they make a face and probably never come back.

Dumper picks up the trash. He carries the can so that the people who are out this Sunday all dressed up have to dodge and jump out of the way. But wait! Dumper's nostrils are opening and shutting. There's something on the sidewalk! He drops the trash can right where everybody's walking and bangs into a lady who is wearing a veil and carrying a lot of parcels. Dumper pounces on something and picks it up off the sidewalk. It's a cent! One cent! Dumper found a cent! Dumper nearly knocked over a bunch of innocent people but he got the cent before they did! Nice going Dumper!

Dumper dumps the trash into the back of his truck. Now he's going to change my grease. Mr. Fryday uses vegetable oil. The vegetable oil is healthier than lard. Mr. Fryday always leaves an empty vegetable oil can near the window so his customers can see it. On the side of the can it says "Cholesterol Free."

Dumper comes around with a large empty grease can and pushes past some customers with it and climbs into the wagon. Some of the customers leave, because Dumper is so ugly. He squats down to hook up the hose to the spigot at the bottom of the blancher. The oil in the blancher is 225 degrees Fahrenheit. Dumper doesn't even use gloves to touch the pipe which is very hot. Dumper doesn't seem to have any feelings. His big rear end takes up most of the room in the wagon.

His big, low ears are filthy.

When the blancher is empty, he takes the pail of used grease and carries it out to his truck. He hoists up the can and dumps it into his big grease barrel in the back of his truck. Grease slops onto the street.

Then he comes back to empty the cooker which is full of week-old grease at 340 degrees Fahrenheit. While he's waiting for it to drain, guess what he does? He spits on my clean floor!

"Hey, Dumper, watch it," I say. "I spent hours this morning scrubbing this floor." Dumper looks at me with his little, close-together eyes. There's not much room in a chipwagon and his breath is going to knock me over.

"What do ya expect me to do? Swallow it?" says Dumper, pointing at the big gob sticking on the floor. Then he lets out a big laugh. What a sense of humour!

"And look, you're spilling grease all over the place!" I tell him.

"So?" says Dumper, taking off the dripping hose and waving it around and hoisting the slopping grease can out to his truck.

Most of the people in Chinatown are crossing Somerset Street to the other side. They don't even want to be on the same block as Dumper. There's grease on his shoes, on his pants, on his shirt. There's grease on the floor of the wagon, on the windows, across the counter, on the step, on the sidewalk, on the front of the wagon, on the road, and running down the side of the truck. The grease barrel in the back of the truck is almost full. You can tell it's almost full because when he dumps the can, a geyser of grease reaches up out of the barrel and then flops like a wet bedsheet onto Somerset Street.

"Dumper!" I shout, "I'm going to suggest to Mr. Fryday that you're bad for business and that you're a filthy pig!" My mouth again.

"You watch your mouth, sonny!" says Dumper Stubbs, pulling up his pants even higher than they are, "that mouth of yours is goin' to sink you in too deep one of these days!"

Dumper gives me my three new cans of vegetable oil, gets in his truck and pulls away. The grease barrel in the back is slopping grease all over the place. The smoke from his exhaust pipe is blue. His muffler sounds like twenty chain saws.

Dumper is an environmental disaster.

I put on my gloves and remove the hose and close the hot spigots at the bottom of my two fryers. I carefully pour one and a half cans of vegetable oil in each fryer. Then I turn both fryers back on and set the temperatures.

I figure that each fryer in my wagon holds about a kitchen sinkful of cooking grease. Dumper picks up two kitchen sinkfuls of grease from my wagon each week. Mr. Fryday runs ten chipwagons in Ottawa. Each wagon has at least two fryers. In fact, a couple of the bigger wagons have three fryers. And Mr. Fryday is thinking of buying another wagon to add to his collection. I think he said it would be called "Bach's" chips. So, Dumper Stubbs picks up at least more than twenty kitchen sinkfuls of cooking grease a week on his rounds. It fills a huge barrel.

That's a lot of used grease!

I get out my rags and my all-purpose cleaner squirt bottle and clean the grease off the windows and the counter that Dumper sprayed around. Then I get out my squeeze mop and some more cleaning fluid and clean up the floor and the cooker and clean off the bottoms of my shoes.

The customers are starting to come back and I put on Beethoven's First Symphony, the Third Movement, to get Dumper out of my brain.

Soon after things are back to normal and the wagon is sparkling clean again and the music is right and the Sunday in Chinatown is just right and the customers are back to normal, along comes Mr. Fryday and, as usual, he's in a pretty good mood. He's been telling me lately about a song he's been working on to be used on TV and on the radio to advertise his chipwagons. The song is all about Mr. Fryday and how everyday is "Fryday" (get it?) in the chipwagon business. Mr. Fryday is all excited about it. I can tell by the way he's humming parts of it and trying to make it fit with Beethoven's First Symphony, Third Movement. And I know that he wants me to ask him how the song is going, and when is it going to be on TV and on the radio and all that stuff.

"It's going fine," says Mr. Fryday, after I ask him how it's going.

"Do you want to hear some verses I just wrote?" he asks. I'm just about to say, yes, I would like to hear the verse he just wrote, when he tears right into it, drumming the rhythm for it with his fat fingers on the counter:

> Fryday is my day
> Everyday's a fry day
> When you do it my way
> It's a peachy pie day!
>
> Fryday's my high day
> Not to reason why day
> The limit is the sky day
> A come-over-and-say-hi! day
>
> Fryday is my day
> It's a do-or-die day
> So all you gotta do is buy
>   Some French Fries
> All you gotta do is . . .
> What I'm tellin' you is . . .
> Come and have a REAL
>   FRENCH
>   FRY!

Drumming away with his fat fingers on the counter, his rings tapping and flashing in the Somerset Street sunlight in Chinatown.

Trying to make his song fit with Beethoven's First Symphony, Third Movement.

Mr. Fryday will work the rest of today in the wagon until around five or six o'clock, it depends on the customers, and then he'll close up the wagon, turn off the fryers, cover them, and drive the wagon very carefully home to his place and park it in his yard for the night. The other nine wagons are run by nine other men who work for Mr. Fryday. At night, each man drives his wagon home and parks it in his yard or in his laneway until the next day.

Will Mr. Fryday, while he's driving home, tap the steering wheel with the rings on his fingers, practising his potato chip song that he's so proud of?

Maybe. Maybe he will.

And in a couple of years, when I get my licence, maybe I'll be driving the wagon home to my place. Maybe.

I slip out of the wagon and say goodbye to Mr. Fryday. He doesn't answer. Beethoven's First Symphony is on very loud and I can't see if the noodles are jumping and shaking on the shelves of the Mekong Grocery.

And now the customers are all crowded around Mr. Fryday and now the chips are selling like hot cakes.

I run home to where I live at 179 Rochester Street, Apt. D.

My mom, Ellen O'Reilly Sweetgrass, is part Irish and part a whole lot of other things. She's the Multicultural Counsellor at the Community Resource Centre. She has a whole lot of education and is very smart. She's also funny.

Or, at least, she used to be, before my father died. She is also very determined.

Or, at least, she used to be before my father died. One time she wanted to move our fold-out couch that unfolds into a bed to the other room so instead of waiting for my father and me to get home to help her she did it herself. The couch is really a bed and is full of metal and weighs at least a ton. When we got home we couldn't believe she moved it by herself.

"Remember how I always say I'm part Irish and part a whole lot of other things?" she explained that day. "Well, I forgot to mention it but I am, among other things, part dung beetle!"

My father and I laughed for about a half an hour. We all knew what dung beetles were. We used to watch them when we went hiking. A dung beetle can carry a lump of doo about ten times the size of itself. That's all a dung beetle seems to do. Carry lumps of doo doo around the size of houses.

My mother is thin and very strong. She is also very beautiful. She could be a model but she says she's a bit too short.

And she can hold you with her eyes.

Brown eyes with green flecks.

Specially when she tilts her head to one side.

Or, at least she used to, before my father died.

Right now, she's not at home.

She's probably across the street and down a bit, at the Village Inn. She likes it over there because people over there knew my dad, and she feels good when they say his name or even if they don't.

They all know what a good trombone player he was. They all love how he played on the record, "Hanging Gardens." Over at the Village Inn, they have that record on the old-fashioned juke box. My mom drinks rye and ginger ale over there.

My mom feels awful. Ever since my father died. She never laughs anymore. She sits over there in the Village Inn at the same table. There's always that empty seat beside her. She sits over there beside the empty chair, where my father's ghost sits. He said some mean things to her before he died. The doctor said he didn't know what he was saying, because of the cancer in his brain.

She sits beside his ghost over there every day.

Is she waiting for the ghost to say he's sorry?

And she never looks at me anymore the way she used to. With her eyes holding you. And her head tilted. And the little smile.

I put on my bathing suit under my pants, race down the crooked back steps and take out my bike from the old shed.

I sail down Somerset Street hill on my bike to Corso Italia (Preston Street). I swing right on Preston, ride hard to Scott Street, take a fast left on Scott to Parkdale, cut right on Parkdale through Tunney's Pasture and all the government buildings to the Ottawa River Parkway. I take the grass instead of the ramp and head west on the Parkway to Kitchissippi Lookout.

I vault off my bike at the top of the sandy bank near the change houses. Now I can see Connie Pan getting together her group on Westboro Beach.

It's a group of people of many sizes and colours and shapes.

And the beach is crowded with beach freaks.

V

ometimes Westboro Beach is closed because of pollution. But this week it's not closed and today everybody's having fun.

And Connie Pan is organized.

We're going to play E.S.L. volleyball.

First, Connie Pan gets me to make a pile of sand high enough so that when she stands on it she's as tall as I am. It's fun piling up some sand and getting her to stand up on it every two minutes to see if it's high enough yet. At last it's high enough and her cute little nose is right level with my handsome big nose.

Connie Pan's mother says all of us in Canada have big noses. That's why we all look the same.

The pile of sand is for Connie to stand on while she referees the E.S.L. volleyball game.

I will stand six paces across from Connie Pan with one arm up in the air and my hand held out flat. That is how high the net will be. Standing on her pile of sand, Connie Pan also has her arm up and her hand out flat. That will be the other end of the net. In between Connie Pan and me is empty space. It's empty space because we have no net.

When you play E.S.L. volleyball with Connie Pan, you just pretend you have a net.

Connie Pan has a whistle, though. And whenever one of the players touches the net that isn't there, Connie Pan blows her whistle.

There's one other rule about E.S.L. volleyball that's different from ordinary volleyball. In E.S.L. volleyball there's no ball, either.

You just pretend you have a ball.

And Connie Pan is very organized.

Around each player's waist is tied a neat white cloth sign, like a little apron, with the player's name and the player's country printed in magic marker. The printing is neat and perfect. Printing done by the hands of Connie Pan.

On one team is the Pham family from Vietnam: Minh Dang Pham, Minh Duong Pham, Tan Phong Pham and Toan Anh-Ngoc Pham. Also on that team is Ahmed H. Elhagghassan from Lebanon.

It's not fair to have the Pham family all on the same team because they're too good. The way they go around when the ball is up in the air, the way they talk to each other in Vietnamese as it goes higher and higher, and the way they all shade their eyes from the sun at the same time when they see that the ball is starting to come down, and the way they get more and more excited as the ball comes down closer and closer, and then the way they start to argue and shove each other out of the way, each one trying to be the one who gets to hit it. And then the way, at the last minute, they decide by flipping a coin and letting it fall in the sand, which Pham of the Pham family is going to hit the imaginary ball up to Ahmed H. Elhagghassan who will then spike it over the net. They are too good for the other team. They are too good at pretending that there's actually a ball there.

When the Pham family is playing E.S.L. volleyball, most of the Canadians on Westboro Beach think there is a ball up there and there really *is* a net to hit it over!

On the other team: Claudia N. Mejia Escobar from Argentina; Somasundarum Selvakumaram from Sri Lanka; Mussie Waldegeberael from Ethiopia; Chittavong Saravong from Cambodia; the player with the most names, Abdi-Hakum T. Haji-Aden from Somalia; and the player with the shortest name, Ha Ng from Hong Kong.

Ha, the captain of that team, serves first.

Connie Pan blows her whistle.

The ball has touched the net. Ha Ng has to serve it over again. All her team are telling her to serve it higher. The Pham family on the other side of the net are all laughing. She'll never get it over the net, they are saying.

Ha serves again. This one is a high one. The Pham family are staggering backwards, backwards, backwards. Look at it go! They all fall backwards right into the Ottawa River! Out of bounds! Ha's team loses the serve.

For the other team, Ahmed H. Elhagghassan serves. As the ball goes up, the Pham family each points in a different direction. Where is the ball? The Pham family is acting like the ball is in four different places! But wait, Claudia N. Mejia Escobar is under it, she sets it for Somasundarum Selvakumaram who spikes it down the Pham family's throat!

Change of serve.

For Ha's team we have Abdi-Hakum T. Haji-Aden serving. Abdi points high in the air. He will serve a very, very high one. He serves it. Up it goes. The Pham family are silent. They follow the ball up into the sun, shading their eyes. Up it goes further, further, until the Pham family's necks get sore looking up. To rest their necks, they lie on the sand and watch, lying on their backs in the sand, watching the ball go further up into the sky.

But, look!

It's starting to come down. The Pham family is up. Now they are running around in a circle, shouting stuff in Vietnamese. Faster, faster they run in the circle as the ball gets closer and closer. All of a sudden they stop running. They each shake hands with Toan Anh-Ngoc Pham, who is the captain. They step back and bow to him. He gets set, his knees bent, his fingers ready. Here it is! He's under the ball perfectly, lifting it just right so that Ahmed H. Elhagghassan can spike it over the net. Score! Everybody on Ha's team falls down. What a play!

The Pham family serves again.

The ball is returned by Chittavong Saravong. Another very, very high one. The Pham family watches it sail up. They flip a pretend coin to see who will get it. Tan Phong Pham wins. He will be the one. But wait. Tan has to go to the toilet. He's wiggling and writhing and touching himself. Well, hurry up, they say. Go! Tan runs up the hill to the change house and disappears in the toilet.

Everybody on Westboro Beach is waiting.

Now the Pham family is starting to yell up to the toilet and they're also looking at their pretend watches and saying to the crowd on Westboro Beach, where is he? Why is he taking so long? Now they're yelling harder, because the ball is on its way down. Hurry, Tan, hurry! The Pham family is going crazy now, they can hardly stand it. Please Tan, get out here! This ball is almost here!

All of a sudden, Tan is at the door of the toilet. He's backing out, pulling on his bathing suit. The crowd on Westboro Beach is roaring and shouting for him to hurry. Never mind your bathing suit! Tan is running now, pulling his bathing suit up under his apron with his name and his country printed on by Connie Pan's careful hands.

Hurry! Hurry!

The Pham family lets out a long terrifying wail. Will it be too late? Tan dives in, just in time, his bathing suit half off, and lifts the ball perfectly to Ahmed H. Elhagghassan. Ahmed spikes it down so hard that the other team doesn't even see it.

The Pham family goes nuts.

After about an hour of this, Connie Pan blows the whistle and everybody goes swimming.

It is the best volleyball game ever! Everybody on Westboro Beach is laughing and the kids are all trying to imitate the Pham family, specially the part where they run around bumping into each other while they're looking up into the air, shading their eyes, trying to see the ball up there, waiting for the ball to start to come down. But the kids aren't as good as the Phams, of course, because there's always one kid who gets impatient and who hits the ball too soon and then they all start hitting the ball and arguing and wrestling and falling down. And then there's no ball at all.

And over on another part of Westboro Beach a kid's mother is making an apron out of string and cardboard and helping her kid put his name on it and the country he's from, and helping him tie it around his waist. The sign says, "Jim Smith, Canada."

I help unpile the sand that Connie Pan was standing on and we make the beach even again. Then she makes me help her fold up the invisible net, very neatly, until I have it folded across my arms. I'm very embarrassed doing this because I feel silly and because I'm not a very good actor and there's a bunch of little kids standing around watching with their mouths hanging open.

Then Connie Pan takes the invisible net off my arms and folds it into a smaller piece and then into a smaller piece and then it's small enough to go into her hands and then tiny enough to go into one hand, and then she opens up her hand over her head like she's letting go a little bird and she blows on her hand. And the net is gone.

What a volleyball game!

What happened to the ball?

The Pham family decided that it never came down!

That's why the game was over.

Later, Connie Pan and I are up to our chins in the water. Connie Pan is standing on the bottom and I'm kneeling on the bottom.

We're watching the beach. Watching the Canadians and the new Canadians fooling around and lying around the sand. I notice that every few minutes Mussie Waldegeberael, from Ethiopia, is looking up at the sky.

"He waits and hopes for the ball to fall down," says Connie Pan, a little bit of sadness in her voice.

Then Connie Pan and I start talking about her parents and how they don't like me and how, since

I got kicked out of Ottawa Tech, they don't like me even worse. And Connie Pan is saying how her parents don't like the "round-eyes" and stuff like that, which is making me feel sad. Now Connie Pan is telling me that she liked me the day I chased the guys away from bugging the Muslim on his rug that time and that makes me feel good again. But now I'm sort of not listening to what she's saying anymore because something is grabbing my mind away.

What is it?

What is wrong with me?

It's the water. It's that smell on the top of the water. There it is again!

It can't be, but it is!

I smell potato chips!

I smell rancid potato chips here in the water of the Ottawa River at Westboro Beach!

How can that be?

Is it grease up my nose from working in a chipwagon too long? Feel the water. It feels greasy!

Grease in the water at wonderful Westboro Beach!

Disgusting!

VI

D ink the Thinker is fidgeting around my wagon. His foxy face is all over the place. He's moving the trash pail, picking up the salt and putting it down, dropping a drop of vinegar on his finger and licking it, staring at my customers while they wait for their orders to come out, sighing when they can't find their money, rolling his eyes when another customer shows up, counting the funny-looking vegetables in the boxes lined along Somerset Street in front of the Mekong Grocery, kicking the tires of my truck.

I know what's wrong with Dink the Thinker. He's got something important to tell me. He can hardly wait. And I know what he's going to do. He's going to make me guess what it is that he can't wait to tell me.

He takes my picture with his imaginary camera.

It's lunchtime and Somerset Street is busy. My wagon is in front of the Mekong Grocery. Down Somerset Street there is Pacific Video, the Sunshine Coin Wash, Valentino's Strip Club, Vietnamese Sub, Chinese Traditional Acupuncture and Hong Kong Computers.

Up Somerset Street there's the Shahi Tandi Indian Cuisine, the Bangkok Grocery, the Noodle Express Restaurant, Mee Fung Pastry, the Chinese Fashion Corner. Then Bell Street and Arthur Street and the Hong Kong Beauty Salon where Connie Pan works part time.

Dink the Thinker can't wait. Even though there's two customers waiting, Dink can't.

"Guess who I saw going into Valentino's?" says Dink. Valentino's is just down Somerset Street across from the Lao Thai Grocery and Fax store. In Valentino's, while you're eating your lunch or drinking beer, a woman will climb up on your table and take all her clothes off.

One time last summer, Dink and I ran in the front door of Valentino's and out the back door while the waiters ran all around trying to catch us. We were in there just long enough for our eyes to get used to the dark.

It was just like I said.

Men sitting at tables drinking beer and women with no clothes on dancing on the tables.

Well, not exactly no clothes on, Dink the Thinker said; they had shoes on. And one of them had glasses on.

Dink always has to get everything exactly right. Like, if you said to him one day in November, "Look Dink, all the leaves are off the trees," he'd probably say. "Well, not exactly. There's one leaf hanging on to the top of that maple tree, see, over there?"

"Come on, guess," says Dink. "Guess who I saw going into Valentino's?"

"Dumper Stubbs," I guess.

"Wrong," says Dink. "Guess again."

"Mr. Fryday," I guess again.

"Wrong," says Dink. "Guess again."

The thing about Dink is that even though he can't wait to tell you, he'll make you guess all day long unless you force him to tell you or bribe him.

"Captain James T. Kirk of the Star Ship Enterprise," I say.

"Wrong. Guess again."

"Control agent Maxwell Smart. I don't know, Dink. Tell me. Who?"

"What's it worth to you?"

"How would you like one order of Beethoven's Classical Fries, on the house?"

"Sold. On the wagon, you mean."

Picky picky. On the house. On the wagon. Sometimes Dink the Thinker can bug you.

"It was your favourite teacher, the famous hot shot, Mr. Boyle," says Dink. "I took his picture. It was perfect. Imagine, if I had a real camera?"

I give him the fries and pretend to take his money because a customer is coming.

Funny how you're always surprised when you hear of a teacher doing stuff like drinking beer and getting naked women to stand on his table. Or you hear of priests doing stuff. It can sort of make you sick.

All of a sudden something comes rushing into my head. I can see myself standing outside Valentino's when Mr. Boyle comes out. And guess what I see myself, hear myself say to him? I say, "You do that at home all the time." Sort of like on "Jeopardy!" The answer first. And then Boyle gives the question. "Do what at home?"

"Get women with no clothes on to stand on the table while you're sitting there drinking beer."

It's one of those things that you have to imagine because it never happens. Who ever gets to pay back his teacher like that?

Who ever gets to catch the teacher, who got him kicked out of school, coming out of a place where women take off all their clothes except their shoes and stand on his table while he's drinking beer?

I change the subject. I tell Dink all about yesterday's E.S.L. volleyball game and how all the players liked Connie Pan the way she did everything. I don't tell Dink all about how I liked Connie Pan the way she did everything magic with the net and the whistle and her printing on the aprons and the invisible ball and her little hands and her cute nose and my big nose that her mother said made all Canadians look the same.

Now, my regular customers start coming around; the waiter with the piece out of his ear from the Nha Hang Vietnam Restaurant just down the street and the owner of the Wah Shing Gifts and Pots Store across the street and another regular customer, the doctor from the Acupuncture Clinic who always wears the straw hat and the girl from Asia Video across the street and the guy who sets up the balls at the Vietnamese Pool Hall, who looks like his pants are going to fall down any minute now.

Then along comes Connie Pan on her lunch break from her part-time job up at the Hong Kong Beauty Salon and right away Dink can't wait to tell her who he saw going into Valentino's for lunch today.

"Guess who I saw going into Valentino's today," he says to Connie Pan.

For some reason or other I don't want Dink to start talking about that in front of Connie Pan.

Maybe it's because she'd be embarrassed or shy about a subject like that or maybe it's because I don't want Dink to tell her that we ran through there last summer with the waiters chasing us, just to see what it was like. I don't want Connie Pan to know I did that.

So I change the subject.

I start telling Connie Pan and Dink and the guy from the Bangkok Grocery up the street, who is standing around eating his fries, all about Mr. Fryday's song and how he wants it to go on TV and on the radio. Beethoven's Symphony No. 5 is on, the Second Movement, playing nice and quiet. I've got it turned down low.

We're having a very nice time.

Then I start telling them all about how when Mr. Fryday first started in the chip business he parked his wagon right in front of a restaurant on Rideau Street and got into big trouble with everybody. What happened was, people were buying potato chips from Mr. Fryday's wagon and then taking them into the restaurant and sitting there with a glass of water and eating the chips. They were even using the restaurant's salt and vinegar which was on the table, and, like the owner was shouting to the cops after, even using his ketchup and his serviettes and his forks!

So the owner started kicking the people out of his restaurant and a fight started out on the street because the owner pushed one of them and spilled her chips on the sidewalk and she said the restaurant guy should buy her some new chips because she hardly had eaten any of them. And he said she only had a few left in the bottom and her boyfriend said are you pushing my girlfriend and punched the restaurant guy in the mouth. Then Mr. Fryday got out of his wagon and the dishwasher from the restaurant and two waiters came out and a big brawl started and Mr. Fryday had his pants ripped right off him. And somebody threw a restaurant ashtray through the window of Mr. Fryday's truck. And a bunch of punkers came out of the Video Arcade next door and were rocking Mr. Fryday's wagon trying to tip it over when the cop cars came screaming up.

That's why Mr. Fryday never parks in front of a restaurant. There's all kinds of restaurants in Chinatown on Somerset Street in Ottawa and Mr. Fryday's wagon is parked between them, not in front of any of them.

I give Connie Pan a loonie and ask her to feed the meter for me.

I like the way she takes the loonie in between her thumb and forefinger and slips it in the meter. Then twists the handle.

We're having a nice time.

But, all of a sudden everything is ruined.

Because here comes Dumper Stubbs in his filthy truck with the big ugly steel bumper on the front to pick up the trash.

When he dumps my trash he hits the can against his grease barrel and it makes a dull, heavy clunking sound.

It's like my dad used to say. You're having a lovely garden party and a skunk shows up!

After everybody leaves it gets quiet and I start Beethoven's Fifth at the beginning of the First Movement.

Purple clouds are rolling in and the sky coming over from the west is black. There's a wind blowing dirt and papers up in the air. A woman goes by holding her veil with one hand and her long dress with the other.

For the first two movements of Beethoven's Symphony No. 5 to play on my disc player in my wagon it takes exactly seventeen minutes and fifteen seconds.

Exactly seventeen minutes and fifteen seconds after I start Beethoven's Fifth Symphony, I see Mr. Boyle coming up the street from Valentino's towards my wagon. As he gets closer I can see he's staggering a bit. The wind is giving him a bad time. The kind of wind you get in the hot summer after a long heat wave and before a big storm on Somerset Street in Chinatown in Ottawa.

I can tell he's not going to see me here in my wagon. He's going to walk right by. Unless I do something.

I turn up the volume until I figure the noodles on the shelves in the Mekong Grocery must be trembling.

Then, just as he's passing my window, I shut Beethoven completely down. The jolt snaps his head around but he still can't see me.

I shout. I shout the answer.

"You do that at home all the time!"

He stops but he still doesn't seem to know where the voice is coming from.

I shout again.

"You do that at home all the time!"

He looks right at me in my wagon.

There's steam swirling around me in the window. He's squinting a bit. There's thunder rumbling. The thunder crashes. The crash seems to open his eyes. He sees me now. He figures out who it is. He figures out what I'm saying.

I crank the Beethoven up as far as I can without blowing my speakers.

I yell.

"How are the naked women doing today? At Valentino's. The naked women on the tables. How are they today?"

His whole face changes. His teacher's face grows over his real face. I can see his face changing, just like you see sometimes in a movie, a man's face changing right before your eyes! Trick photography!

"Sweetgrass!" he shouts. "John Sweetgrass! I didn't know you worked in a chipwagon! How long have you worked in a chipwagon? Maybe I should buy some chips from you!"

I hate the sound of my name when it comes out of Boyle's mouth.

I shout.

"We're not getting off on the wrong foot are we!"

The last movement of Beethoven's Fifth is crashing away.

The sky dumps a lake of rain on us. A bolt of lightning stabs into Somerset Street in front of the Chinese Clinic.

Mr. Boyle is suddenly soaking wet. His shirt is hanging wet over his ugly beer gut. His face is red and he's spitting spit and rain. He's shouting something at me. Something, something "you punk!"

Something, something "you punk!"

"We're closed!" I shout, and slam shut the window.

The two magic words, followed by "you punk!" The first word is the one used in the same way in every language on earth by everybody, according to Dink the Thinker.

The other word is "you."

It takes exactly eight minutes and fifty-seven seconds for Beethoven to get through the Fourth Movement of Symphony No. 5.

It takes about the same time to fill Somerset Street with a roaring river of rain in a wild summer storm.

I turn the keys in the ignition and switch on the wipers. The wagon is fogged in. I have to clear a space on the windshield with my hand so I can watch the storm.

The rain is roaring down Somerset Street from up around the Yangtze Restaurant. It's a swollen, slashing, swirling river of rain, sucking down the storm sewers and filling the roadway up over the curbs.

Beethoven is competing with the thunder and lightning. The rain is whipping from the sky like a vicious curtain in the wind. The signs of the shops of Chinatown are lifting and bending and swinging and rattling and screaming.

The water is roaring down past Jasmine's Sports Bar and the Golden River Restaurant, past the Caisse Populaire St. Jean Baptiste Chinese Bank, past the Somerset Heights Community Police Centre over Lebreton Street, past the International Driving School, the Chinese Typesetters, the Asia Pizza, over Booth Street, past the India Food Centre, the Reggae Club, the Sun Ming Meat and Seafood Company and under my wagon.

Dresses that were hanging outside the Indian Fashions Shop are flying over the chimneys like witches.

A box of funny-looking vegetables floats by.

The stoplight at Booth Street is swinging wild like a broken lighthouse in a typhoon.

The guy at the Bangkok Grocery is trying to drag a box of cabbages into his store. The wind catches his door and it smashes back against his live-fish tank. The tank collapses and smashes. The fish swim out the door and take off down Somerset Street. A huge carp swims past my wagon.

Free at last!

Some smashed flat Chinese ducks float around in a whirlpool over a storm sewer.

A chain of lightning splits the street and an explosion of thunder knocks Chinatown in half.

Beethoven's in his big finish and the timpani drums are pounding and the cymbals are crashing and the horns are blowing and howling and the fiddles are racing away and the rain is slashing down and Chinatown is floating.

All of a sudden it stops. I open my window.

There is only light rain falling.

Beethoven's not finished, though. He's in his last minute of his Fifth Symphony. Boom! Boom! Boom!

Beethoven wins! What a way to do a storm!

There's no sign of Mr. Boyle. Maybe he's been sucked down a sewer.

I wish!

VII

I hear my mom get up and then phone somebody and then go back to bed. I know who
she's phoning. She's phoning work.

I make her a cup of instant coffee and take it
into her bedroom. She's not feeling good this morning so she phoned in sick. She was out late last
night at the Village Inn.

We have a little chat about what we always have
a chat about. My father.

"There's a lot of your father in you, John," she
is saying. "He was a stubborn, outspoken man. It
caused him a lot of trouble. And it could cause you
trouble. Remember that."

This little chat makes me feel very empty inside.
We're not talking the way we used to. We're talking
about him all the time. All the time comparing me
to him. And all bad stuff. She's looking at me but I
don't feel it.

And another thing.

I feel very sneaky and guilty.

Because she doesn't know they kicked me out of
school.

I never told her.

Things just aren't the same anymore.
I used to tell her everything.
Now, I don't tell her anything.
Well, too bad.
She doesn't tell me anything either.
So, I guess you could say we're even.

I go down the back stairs and get my bike out of the shed. It's early and I'm going to go over to Mr. Fryday's house and help him get the wagon ready. He lives over on Bayswater Avenue. I also want to talk to him about a couple of things.

I speed up Rochester Street, turn left at Somerset, sail down Somerset on over the bridge over the City Centre and turn left on Bayswater. Bayswater is a nice street with trees and houses with verandahs and yards. And cats in the windows.

I turn into Mr. Fryday's laneway and lean my bike on the end of his long verandah with the pillars. On the verandah is Mrs. Fryday, sitting in her white chair at a little white table having her breakfast. Mrs. Fryday is an invalid and Mr. Fryday has to take care of her. He comes out the screen door and puts an icing sugar covered doughnut on a plate on her little table. The doughnut is cut up in small pieces so she can eat it. She has a glass of iced tea with a straw in.

Mr. Fryday and I go into the yard and start to get the truck ready. While I'm spraying the windows with vinegar and water and cleaning them I discuss with Mr. Fryday the first thing I want to talk to him about. It's about the cardboard sign he uses in the truck. One side of the sign says "Sorry, We're Closed" and the other side says "Come In, We're Open!" I want Mr. Fryday to change the sign. First of all, what's the use of saying "Sorry, We're

Closed." When a chipwagon is closed, it's driving along a street or it's parked in somebody's yard.

And the other side of the sign is useless, too. "Come In, We're Open!" You can't come in a chipwagon. You stay outside a chipwagon.

Mr. Fryday and I discuss changing, getting a better sign, having no sign at all. Maybe you don't need a sign on a chipwagon.

While I help fill the salt shakers and vinegar bottles and wipe off the counters with baking soda, Mr. Fryday goes and helps Mrs. Fryday back in the house to wait for the person who comes over to take care of her for the rest of the day.

While I'm cleaning the Beethoven CDs with special fluid to keep the grease from spoiling the music, Mr. Fryday gets in the truck and starts the motor. While he's carefully backing the wagon out of his laneway, I get my bike and wait at the curb on Bayswater Avenue. When Mr. Fryday's truck is backed onto the street and ready to go, I pull my bike alongside and hold onto his outside mirror. We take off slowly. I always wish Mr. Fryday would drive a little faster but I guess he never will. He's the most careful driver in the world.

And he always drives with his parking lights on.

While I hang on to the driver's side and while the cars blow their horns and rip around us squealing their tires, we swing up over onto Wellington Street to get into the City Centre where the Potato Processing Plant is, almost under the bridge. Mr. Fryday buys all his potatoes here.

"It's very commendable that you take such an interest in the business, Spud Sweetgrass," Mr. Fryday is saying to me, talking loud so that I can hear him over the squealing of the tires and the honking of the horns of the impatient cars behind us.

"I'm going to think about what you said about the signs. I have the identical sign in all ten of my wagons, so if I decide to make a change, it will be an important and expensive decision. I want you to do a little research for me, if you can. Find me a better idea for a sign, one that's not too expensive and I'll consider it. Perhaps there will even be a little bonus or a commission in it for you. I agree with you. It is silly to have a sign on a chipwagon, saying 'Come In, We're Open!' when you don't mean it. Why didn't I notice that! Well done, Spud. You'll go far in the chip business one day!"

We pull up in front of the Potato Processing Plant almost under the Somerset Street Bridge. Even outside here, we can hear the potatoes thundering.

We go in.

Mr. Fryday is talking to the manager in his little glass office, talking about old potatoes and new potatoes, about animal grease and vegetable oil, about restaurants and chipwagons, about hiring people, people who are good workers, people who aren't.

I can see Mr. Fryday pointing over to me with his thumb. Mr. Fryday likes me. He thinks I'm a good worker, a smart person. A co-operative person. A bit mouthy maybe, at times, but a good lad. And he liked my father a lot.

Mr. Fryday does not know that I got hoofed out of school this May just before exams. I never told him. I guess I'm ashamed of it. Or, maybe it's none of his business.

I go around the Potato Processing Plant, following the potatoes around. They start up above on a platform in bags. The guy up there cuts open a bag and the potatoes go thundering and bouncing down the chute and then fall on a moving ramp that moves uphill so that all the mud and dirt and stones get knocked off the potatoes while they try their best to get to the top.

After they tumble and work and ride to the top they fall over the edge, just like kids in my class going out the door of Mr. Boyle's room. They fall into a big metal drum, booming and echoing like Beethoven. Here the big ones go into one peeler and the small ones into another peeler. They roll around between rollers in there, rollers that look like they are covered with coarse sandpaper. Now they come back out white and peeled and two guys pick up the potatoes and gouge them out with little ice cream scoops and let the little potato balls fall down another ramp. The little potato balls are for fancy restaurants.

Then most of the potatoes go through the chipper. The chipper sounds like the machine the tree cutters on the street use to grind up the branches and twigs and leaves of the tree they just cut. Then the chips come falling and tumbling out and splash into a white foamy bubble tub bath of chemicals to keep them from turning black like an apple does if you bite into it and then leave it on the table all morning.

Then they get drained on another ramp and then they go into a bagger and get bagged and weighed.

I go back to the little office and wait for Mr. Fryday to finish his business with the manager.

Today's *Ottawa Citizen* is sitting there on the bench. I see the words Westboro Beach on the front page. I can't help it, but right away, as soon as I see those two words, Westboro Beach, a picture of Connie Pan pops onto the screen of my mind. The picture is of Connie Pan, up to her chin in water.

But wait! What does the paper say about Westboro Beach? I read a few more words. Westboro Beach closed. Pollution. Water unsafe. Authorities. Further notice. And other words like that. My mind is running up and down like the potatoes trying to get up the ramp. Try to get up. Fall back down. Crawl up again. Roll back down. This time. This time!

I'm back out holding on to the outside mirror, riding slowly along Corso Italia, turning left to go carefully up Somerset Street hill, stopping and carefully parking in front of the Mekong Grocery.

Like I always do, I remind Mr. Fryday to switch off his parking lights. He always forgets.

I turn on my cookers and set out the containers. I put up my display and turn the cardboard sign over to the side that says "Come In, We're Open!"

I get a bag of fresh-cut potatoes that we picked up from the Processing Plant and set it in the corner on the counter. I put out the "no cholesterol" empty vegetable oil can where the customers can see it. I put on Beethoven's Sixth Symphony, very low. There won't be any customers for maybe an hour yet. Lots of time. Maybe I'll get Dink to get me an *Ottawa Citizen* when he comes along. Maybe read the news about Westboro Beach again. How they closed it because of pollution. The picture of Connie Pan pops onto the screen of my mind again. I see both Connie Pan and me in the picture this time. The camera moves in closer. Closer to Connie Pan's mouth. Closer to my nose. Closer to the minute when I tasted the water.

Mr. Fryday is getting ready to leave on his rounds. He's very happy, humming and trying out his Fryday song under his breath, polishing his rings while he's humming.

"Have a successful Fry-day, Spud Sweetgrass," says Mr. Fryday, "sell those chips like hot cakes!"

"Mr. Fryday," I say, "there's another thing I wanted to say to you today. Another thing I thought you might want to discuss besides the 'Come In, We're Open!' sign."

"Discuss away, Spud Sweetgrass! Always glad to learn from and listen to an industrious and bright representative of our younger generation!"

"The other day I was swimming at Westboro Beach and I could smell and even taste chip grease in the water," I say.

Mr. Fryday's face changes.

"Do you think," I say, "that somebody would go down there to the beach and throw worn-out grease in the river?"

Mr. Fryday's face is all of a sudden different than his real face.

How can a person have a new face all of a sudden? Have one face for ever since you met him and then, in one or two seconds, get a brand new face? A darker face. A worried, scared, mad face. Mr. Fryday's fingers go to his cheek. His rings sparkle as they come across his mouth.

VIII

Somerset Street is very quiet this morning. There's nobody in the Mekong Grocery except the guy and his wife who own the place. Pacific Video isn't open yet. The Nha Hang Vietnamese Restaurant has only a couple of customers.

Across the street, at the Wah Shing Gifts and Pots Store, the girl is sweeping the three cement steps.

Into the Sun Ming Meat and Seafood Company a guy is quietly carrying a heavy box. The Palace Dining Lounge is closed until tonight. A woman and a kid are going into the Acupuncture Clinic.

An old man sitting on the steps of the Vietnamese Pool Hall is smoking a cigarette. The guy whose pants are going to fall down any minute now is standing in the doorway.

It's going to be hot again today.

Beethoven's Sixth Symphony is playing very low. If you walk along the Ottawa River Parkway along the bicycle path there, or you walk around Pink Lake up the Gatineau Parkway, the water and the trees and the earth and the sky remind you of Beethoven's Sixth Symphony.

Mr. Fryday's own face is back again. His face of fear is gone. For a little minute there, his new face scared me. And it made me sad. It's sad to see a happy face turn into a face of fear.

"That's a very interesting observation," says Mr. Fryday. "Very interesting. Very serious, too. Suggesting that somebody takes grease down to Westboro Beach and, for some reason, dumps it there."

"Why would anybody do a thing like that?" I say. The guy across the street at the Meat and Seafood Company clatters against the door with his heavy box.

"Could we go down there to Westboro Beach?" says Mr. Fryday. "And could you show me exactly what it is . . . what you think is there?"

"Yes," I say.

"Lock up the wagon," orders Mr. Fryday, and goes into the Mekong Grocery to phone a taxi. In a few minutes along comes a taxi. As soon as we're in the back seat Mr. Fryday is talking away with the driver. The driver is wearing a big beautiful turban. What is his country? How long has he been in Canada? What does his turban mean? Has he got any kids? Does he ever go back to India? How many times? Is it expensive? How many turbans has he got?

By the time we get to Westboro Beach Mr. Fryday knows everything about the guy. He even knows all about a big Sikh party that's coming up. The guy's son, who's going to turn thirteen, will have a huge turban party. Hundreds of people will go. His son will get his first turban and become a man. He will also get his ceremonial dagger. Mr. Fryday gets invited to the party afterwards. Not the ceremony. But the party afterwards.

We get out of the cab and Mr. Fryday gives the guy a big tip. His name is Rajinderpal. Mr. Fryday is his new friend. He's already calling him "Raj."

"Goodbye, Raj, my friend. I'll give you a call!"

"Goodbye, Mr. Fry," shouts Raj, as he drives back onto the Parkway and leaves us at the Kitchissippi Lookout.

We walk past the cement change house where one of the Pham family went to the toilet in the middle of the greatest volleyball game ever. We walk carefully down the bank and step onto Westboro Beach. We are the only people here.

As we get closer to the shore the air seems to get heavy. The river is very calm this morning. It's like blue glass right across to the Quebec shore. Except at the edge it's not blue. It's a yellowish brown colour. Clots of foam sit along the shore. Gobs like the one Dumper Stubbs spit on my floor the other day float near the edge. Except these are the size of garbage pail lids.

A thick cake of brown curd crawls along under the surface all along the beach. On the sand are gummy clotted curdles of brown cream. The booms for the little kids are dripping in lardy fat and blubbery oil. Mouldy rot and filthy slop and scum float out to the rafts. Thick, foul, rancid, rotten, maggoty cheese curls lie in circles around the buoys. Sludge and slush fester and stink and smear and stain the scabby surface. The rocks at the end of the beach are covered with poisonous sores and pus.

And the sand we're standing on feels gummy.

We walk along the shore past the beach. Packs of sickly green moss hang along the rocks. Some of the branches of the trees touch the water. The leaves are hanging in slime. Mr. Fryday bends over and puts his finger in the Ottawa River. He pulls it out and puts it up to his nose.

He looks around for somewhere to wipe it off. He cleans it on a leaf over his head.

"There's something terribly wrong here, Spud Sweetgrass," says Mr. Fryday, almost whispering. We walk further along the shore beyond the beach and sit on a big piece of driftwood back from the water. There's empty beer cans and a burnt-out fire. A big plastic bleach bottle is sitting in the bushes.

"Do you smell it?" I say to Mr. Fryday.

"I smell many things," says Mr. Fryday. "And one of the things I smell smells a lot like rancid cooking grease. What are you thinking, Spud?"

"I don't want to say," I say. "Stubbs, maybe?"

"Are you thinking that my maintenance man, Stubbs, is coming down here in the middle of the night and pouring grease into the river?"

"Somebody is," I say. I look out over the water. I don't want to look at Mr. Fryday.

"He takes the grease to the rendering plant. A barrel a week. He picks up from ten wagons. I pay him three dollars per pick-up plus mileage. Thirty dollars a week. He pays fifteen dollars a week to the rendering company who receives it. He gets a receipt each time. He shows me the receipt. His profit is fifteen dollars a week. That's over and above his regular salary that I pay him. Would he come down here with it instead, just to steal fifteen dollars? It wouldn't be worth it. And anyway, I get the receipts. And don't forget, Spud, I'm not the only person in Ottawa who cooks with grease. There are twenty-five or thirty other wagons in the city, plus every restaurant in the city deep-fries food. It could be any number of people committing this crime."

"Somebody is . . ." I say, feeling a bit ashamed.

"Yes, you're right," says Mr. Fryday. "Somebody is. And it would take more than a barrel or two of grease to cause this. Somebody is dumping a lot more than a barrel or two of grease to cause this mess!"

We leave the river and get up onto the Parkway. We cut across the jogging path, cross the long lawns, cut through a gate in the fence and walk up to the corner of Churchill Avenue and Richmond Road. Mr. Fryday goes into the Easy Street Cafe and gets his friend Terry the Greek to phone us a taxi. Mr. Fryday has friends all over Ottawa.

In the taxi I see on the back of the driver's seat his name: H. Ramlochand. Mr. Fryday is talking to him.

"Harvey, have you been back to Guyana this year? Is your girlfriend a Canadian yet? Is she up here in Canada yet?"

Mr. Fryday knows everybody. He could start his own E.S.L. volleyball team.

H. Ramlochand tells Mr. Fryday all about how the girl he wants to marry is coming to Canada in September and how everything's turning out O.K.

"Goodbye, Harvey my friend," says Mr. Fryday. While we're getting out of the taxi and while he's giving him a big tip, he says, "Don't forget to invite me to your wedding!"

Back at the wagon we have another little chat while I heat up the fryers and get ready. I turn up Beethoven's Sixth Symphony, just to get the thought and the smell and the taste and the idea of Westboro Beach out of my brain.

"Do you mind, Spud," says Mr. Fryday, as he's getting ready to go off on his rounds, "do you mind if I give you a little bit of a lecture, a bit of fatherly advice?" I don't say yes or no or nod my head or anything. What's the use? When they say that, you're going to get the advice no matter what you say. What am I going to say, "No, I don't want your advice, thanks very much, keep your advice to yourself?" It would only be a shock to Mr. Fryday and hurt his feelings because he likes me and thinks I'm a nice guy.

He starts right away.

"I knew your father. He was a fine man, a talented, handsome, intelligent man, and a fine trombone player. In fact I went many times to the Penguin Club on Elgin Street to hear him play when he played there with Nebuchadnezzar and the Babylonians' Jazz and Swing Band. And I know you loved your father very much and that he loved you . . ."

I tune Mr. Fryday out for a while while I listen to Beethoven's part where he's by the brook, and where, by the music, you can tell that the water is beautiful and clear and sometimes shallow and sometimes deep. Then I let Mr. Fryday back in.

" . . . it's understandable that you'd be angry and consider Angelo Stubbs an inferior being and assume he was guilty because he's not a very attractive man, not a very intelligent man perhaps . . ." I cut out Mr. Fryday again for a minute by lowering a cold basket of chips into the hot oil which makes a cracking, roaring sound. ". . . but one mustn't judge a book by its cover, and well, Spud, I'm sure you know exactly what I mean and I don't need to say any more . . . you're a good boy and you'll go far in this world, you will."

He sounds like he's finished so I politely point over his shoulder behind him. There's our first customer of the day, waiting there.

All afternoon I think about my father. Mr. Fryday is right. Maybe I am just mad because Dumper Stubbs is alive and my father's not. It just doesn't seem fair, though.

While the chips are selling like hot cakes I'm thinking of the times I went over to the Penguin Club on Elgin Street and sat there and drank cokes while I watched my dad playing the trombone and how the people would all cheer and say "Yes!" after he'd play a solo. And how he would hold the slide so easy, with his thumb and his finger, his wrist really loose, and how he hardly ever had to shoot the slide away out like the other trombone player in the band did. And how everybody gave standing-up applause when they played their main piece, called "Hanging Gardens." My father wrote that one himself.

Just before supper time, when the chip business is over for the day, along comes my friend Dink the Thinker.

Dink listens while I tell him the whole thing. All about the beach and Mr. Fryday's face, and judging a book by its cover and Dumper Stubbs being innocent and the receipts for the grease and Dumper's fifteen-dollar extra profit on the deal. I tell Dink that I think Dumper would do *anything* to make fifteen extra dollars, it wouldn't matter what it was. Didn't I see him almost knock down everybody in Chinatown just to pick up one cent off the street?

There's one thing, though, that Dink the Thinker and I can't figure out. Like Mr. Fryday said, there's lots more than one or two barrels of grease down there in the water. Where did it come from all at once?

Dink says we check out Dumper's truck after supper. Maybe find some clues. Where is Dumper's truck after supper? It's where it is every night after supper Dink tells me. Parked around the Elmdale Tavern which is on Wellington Street across from the Giant Tiger and next to the Colonel Sanders. Dink sees the truck around there often when he's cruising around on his bike. Dink's eyes are shining like a fox's eyes.

Good idea, Dink, you Thinker!

We go over to Dink's place on Eccles Street and help Dink's dad make the supper. We make roasted cheese and tomato sandwiches in their oven toaster. Dink's dad has a line of vitamin pills in front of his open-face roasted cheese and tomato. To watch Dink's dad eat, you'd think he was a health nut. He gobbles up about twenty different types of vitamin pills and washes them down with a glass of some kind of special health juice that looks like he just scooped it out of the river down at Westboro Beach.

There's only one thing wrong with Dink's dad's health program.

He smokes.

While he's gobbling the pills and washing them down, he's puffing away on a cigarette. While he's eating his roasted tomato and cheese, he's smoking another cigarette. Now, he's got two cigarettes going at once. One is in the ashtray, the other one is in his hand. When he sees the one in the ashtray, he gets a bit embarrassed and puts it out. He puts it out hard, smashing it against the bottom, pounding it to bits on the bottom of the ashtray, like he hates it.

"Another twenty-five cents down the tube," he says. But in the middle of the word "tube" he starts this Olympic coughing attack. He coughs so hard that he has to grab the table with both hands. His face gets a purple colour and his mouth is open like a fish you just pulled out of the water, his tongue is curled into a roll, his eyes are fogged over, his body is doubled up.

Then he gets his breath back and swallows a few times. Then his face is almost back to normal and he lets go of the table. Then he gives us some advice.

"Never smoke, boys!" he says. "Cigarettes will cost you at least twenty-five cents apiece and it's gonna be a lot more by the time the goody-goody busybodies get through with it and anyway, it's bad for your health!"

While he's trying to say the word "health" another coughing fit attacks him, and Dink and I, we take our sandwiches into the other room.

Later, Dumper's truck is there just like Dink said it would be. It's parked around the corner from the Elmdale Tavern on Melrose in front of the famous Takahashi Martial Arts Centre.

When it's dark enough, we climb on.

The barrel in the back is full of grease. There are trash cans and rope and empty boxes and hoses.

The barrel stands about half-way back. If you tipped it, it would just reach the end. The grease would pour out over the back. It would take a very strong person to tip a big barrel like this if it was full to the brim with grease. Dumper is a pretty strong guy. If the truck was parked on a slope, say backed down a beach, it would be easy. You could probably kick it over. It would be quick and easy.

The cab of the truck is filthy and smells like rancid grease. The seat is ripped and there's take-out junk all over the floor. In a slob truck like this, there's one surprising thing.

The glove compartment is locked.

Why does a slob like Dumper Stubbs lock his glove compartment?

Somebody's coming. I hear Dumper's voice. And another man's. Dink and I slip out of the cab and squeeze the door quietly shut. We hide in the laneway in back of the Elmdale Tavern. Here comes Dumper. And who's with him?

It's Mr. Fryday!

Dumper gets in his truck and says something like "see ya" and Mr. Fryday strolls up Wellington Street towards Bayswater, calling out, "Goodnight! Goodnight!"

Dumper's truck takes off in a cloud of pollution that you can see swirling around, even in the dark!

What's Mr. Fryday doing, hanging out with Dumper?

"Doesn't look good for nice Mr. Fryday," says Dink.

I ride along with Dink past my street and over to Dink's. We talk for a while outside his house. Now and then you can hear Dink's dad in there coughing in bed.

Dink goes in and I ride on to Cambridge Street and stop under the street light in front of Connie Pan's house. I'm feeling kind of lonesome and, I guess, I'm hoping Connie Pan will look out the window and see me there.

There's a light on in a room upstairs and I wonder if Connie Pan's up there reading or something.

Maybe I shouldn't be here, specially under the light. What if Mrs. Pan looks out and sees me? Might get Connie Pan in trouble.

The street light is making a perfect shadow of me and my bike on the road.

The part of the shadow that I notice the most, if I move my head a certain way, is my big Canadian nose!

IX

Connie Pan and Dink and me.

And Dink's new camera. A real camera, this time.

Should be a pretty good picnic. Dink has a bag of cheese and tomato sandwiches that his dad made for us. I'm not going to eat any of them in case his dad coughed all over them while he was making them. Connie Pan has egg and mayonnaise and lettuce sandwiches. I'm going to love eating those sandwiches because she made them herself. She also has six huge almond cookies that she bought at the Yangtze Restaurant just up the street from her place. I've got macaroni and cheese cold meat sandwiches, some with ketchup on. Some with mustard. Some with mayonnaise. I also have six apples. I guess I eat a lot.

And Dink the Thinker has his new camera that he's been saving for.

Mr. Fryday gave me today off to research a new sign for his wagons. I think he gave me the day off partly because of what I told him about what I suspected about his wonderful employee, "don't judge a book by its cover," Dumper Stubbs. I think Mr.

Fryday is partly mad at me for saying stuff about his pal, his buddy, who he sits all night with in the Elmdale Tavern, and who would *never* do anything like pollute a river just for some extra money! Dumper "who me?" Stubbs!

I think my mouth has got me into trouble again.

First, a day off. Then a couple of days off. Then, every day off!

Maybe Mr. Fryday is starting to fire me.

Anyway, today we're going to drive straight out Bank Street on our bikes.

Connie Pan's mother won't know Connie Pan is with me because there's a big parade and festival and street sale on in Chinatown today to raise money for some poor people around there. There'll be lots of costumes and kites and dragons and music. Her parents will be busy all day. She told them she doesn't want to do all that stuff. She told them she wants to be Canadian, not Chinese.

"They are mad at me," says Connie Pan. "Once a year, Chinese New Year, is enough," says Connie Pan. "But I have Chinese cookies," she says. "Not so Canadian, yet!"

When she laughs I feel like I feel when I imagine Beethoven taking a stroll on the bikepath along the Gatineau Parkway.

If you go straight down Bank Street as far as you can go, you get to the United States of America. We're not going that far today. We're just going to ride for an hour or two. Just till we get to where the village of Manotick is across the river. Just till we get to the grease rendering place around there.

Where Dumper Stubbs supposedly takes the big full barrel of grease every week. Where he supposedly gives the fifteen to the man and where he supposedly gets a receipt each time which he gives to Mr. Fryday.

Supposedly.

Sure.

There aren't that many places to stop along Bank Street for a picnic. I guess Connie Pan is wondering why I didn't pick a better route with more picnic places. I haven't told her my real reason for this trip. To check out Dumper Stubbs's story. Dink the Thinker doesn't care if there aren't very many nice places to stop for a picnic on Bank Street. He's too busy looking around at everything to see what might be good to take a picture of with his new camera.

We could stop at Landsdowne Park for a while but Landsdowne Park isn't really a park, it's mostly cement and pavement. We could stop at the Rideau Canal but maybe it's too early, we've only been driving along on our bikes for about twenty minutes. We could stop at Billings' Bridge along the Rideau River but there's too much traffic and the river stinks around here anyway.

We stop for a minute at the corner of Bank Street and Albion Road but not to picnic. There are a whole lot of velvet paintings for sale here, leaning on benches along the road. Dink takes a picture of one velvet painting of Elvis who sort of looks like Jesus the way he's looking up. Then Dink takes another picture of another velvet painting, this one is of Jesus. Funny thing, he doesn't look as much like Jesus as Elvis does. We could stop in Blossom Park but Blossom Park is not a park and there are no blossoms. It's just houses.

About fifteen minutes later, we decide to stop for a small picnic. Connie Pan is hungry and so am

I. Dink the Thinker picks the spot for the picnic. It's a graveyard. The Hope Cemetery.

We lean our bikes against the gatepost and go in a bit between the graves where there's room to put down our blanket. This is a pretty crowded, full cemetery. There are thousands of dead people in here. Behind the cemetery there's a junk yard. Full of dead machines and dead cars and dead everything. Dink takes a picture of a grave and then opens up his bag of sandwiches and offers Connie Pan one. But I stick my hand out just ahead of his, offering her one of my sandwiches. I don't want her to eat one of Dink's in case you know who coughed nicotine all over it. She could get lung cancer eating one of those sandwiches.

While we're eating and looking around, we notice that the people in the cars going by on Bank Street are looking at us. I guess it looks weird, a picnic in a graveyard.

If my dead father was here now, with his trombone, I would be the happiest guy in the universe. He would play us a quiet tune, his wrist very loose, his finger and thumb holding the slide so tender, his eyes closed, his neck muscles swelling.

But I'm not the happiest guy in the universe.

I hear somebody saying something to me.

It's Connie Pan. She wants to go.

I don't think she's having a very good time.

Dink shows his instant photos of graves and dead cars to us. He tells us how many years it will take for all this stuff to turn to particles. Then he tells us about the Big Bang Theory of the Universe and how everything is just made of rays shooting down on us from quasars from other galaxies. Then he shows us his photos of Elvis and Jesus.

Connie Pan is getting a bit impatient. I should tell her where we're going but I keep putting it off.

"Is there a maybe better place to perform a picnic?" says Connie Pan.

We take off again on our bikes.

Is this what a Canadian picnic is supposed to be like? Maybe Connie Pan would rather stay Chinese after all. Maybe it's more fun on Somerset Street today, chasing after the tails of huge paper dragons. And untangling kites.

Maybe Mrs. Pan is right. Maybe Canadians are stupid.

Down the road a half an hour there's a Hindu Temple. We stop there and put down our blanket. We open up our sandwiches and apples.

"It's nicer here," says Connie Pan.

An angry man in a white suit comes out and kicks us off the grass. We can't stay here. It's against the rules.

We get on our bikes and take off again. While we're driving along, Dink hands me a photograph. In the photograph there's a man in a white suit, pointing, kicking picnickers off his lawn.

Instant replay.

It's ten o'clock when we get to Rideau Road, near the town of Manotick. Two hours away from Chinatown. I turn left onto Rideau Road at the Swiss Inn and Bottoms Up Club. Connie Pan and Dink follow me but they don't want to. Should I explain to them that I want to talk to the grease man at the depot here to see if he knows Dumper Stubbs? To see if Dumper Stubbs really comes out here every week with his huge barrel of rancid grease? Or find out if he does something else with it?

It's too hard to explain. It won't take long anyway. Just ask the guy. Do you know Dumper Stubbs? That's all. Only takes a second. I can explain everything after.

It's hard to breathe on Rideau Road. It's full of dust and smoke and filth. Cement trucks crashing by knock you off the road. Trucks full of hot asphalt blow burning tar fumes in your face. Big tractor trailers with twenty-two wheels blast their diesel horns at you and knock you off your bike. Fire and smoke blow across from the brickyard. Drilling and blasting rock in the quarry breaks your ears. The stink of chemicals and slime from the ditches makes you feel like barfing.

Connie Pan is mad. "This is not the way to have a picnic!" she shouts. "Where is the picnic place, the picnic park?" Her eyes are full of tears from the poison in the air. All around us is broken pipe, weeds, oil, smoke fumes, steam, gas, sludge, cement, burning rubber, steel fences, fires, broken brick, iron, rust, sulphur, dead machines.

What a perfect place for a picnic!

Now, there's a new smell! It fills Rideau Road with heavy air. It's a smell I know. It's the smell of burning hair, rotten food, dirty rivers, maggots, jars of bacon grease with green mould growing across the top, a dead fat rat with beetles running out. The smell of Dumper Stubbs! We're here!

The grease depot!

There's a little shack that's the office for the grease man. There's a field full of grease cans and barrels. There's a truck and a long tractor trailer. There's a guy getting into the tractor trailer. I'm walking over to the guy. My feet are sinking into the greasy ground, sucking out of my own foot-

74

prints in the cooking-fat ground. Dink the Thinker and Connie Pan are standing on the road beside their bikes. They think I'm crazy. I'm pulling my feet out of the grease mud, getting closer to the driver of the tractor trailer.

"Do you know Dumper Stubbs?" I yell.

"Who?" yells the guy.

"Dumper Stubbs!" I yell, "he's got an ugly truck, comes here once a week, drops off grease. . . ."

The diesel engine is roaring like a lost hurricane.

"Can't hear ya!" the guy yells. "Get in!"

I get in. I look over at Connie Pan and Dink.

Dink is taking a picture of me getting into the truck. Connie Pan is looking at me through the filth like I'm a crazy person.

"I have to talk to this man!" I call to her.

"You want to talk, you have to ride!" screams the guy. "I'm late! I'm rolling!"

I get in.

I try to roll up the window to shut out the noise. One of the mufflers is right outside my window. It's rattling and shaking like it's going to explode. My window won't roll up unless you press the glass with your hand while you wind the crank. I decide I'll ride a few blocks with this man and then get out and walk back. He's yelling at me, talking away about Stubbs and a whole lot of stuff. Once the window is up I can hear better.

". . . usually pick up a hitchhiker. Better to have some company on the trip. Ya ever drive one of these big jobs? Twenty-two wheels. This is not a bad job. Drivin' grease around. You know how much grease we've got on board? Sixty drums.

75

Sixty forty-five-gallon drums of grease. That's a lotta deep-fried pogos right, pal! That's a lotta potatoes frites, you know what I mean? A lotta cholesterol! A lotta heart attacks! HA! HA! Here, ya wanna shift gears. We're going into the last gear. Watch how I double clutch. Don't force it. Take it easy. That's it. Just ease it in. No, no, over more towards you. Now down a bit. That's it. See? Easy eh?"

We're barrelling along pretty fast. It's going to be a longer walk back than . . . I'll get out at the first stoplight.

". . . sure, Stubbs, he's my buddy. Known him for years. I see him about once a week, out at the grease depot. What a guy! A real nut case! I went to school with him. Tried to set fire to our English teacher one time. Honest to God. Another time, drove his truck right into the Gatineau River. Bet me fifty bucks. Said his truck could float! Drunker'n a boiled owl that night! Still owes me the fifty. While we're swimmin' to shore he's yelling, 'I didn't bet, I didn't bet!' What a lunatic!

"Sweetgrass eh? What kind of a name's that? Mine's Delaney, Rene Delaney. They all call me Rainy Day. Rainy Day Delaney. I don't know why. 'Cause I like driving in the rain, I think. Spud, is that your nickname? Probably because of the potatoes, right? Got your driver's licence yet? Not yet? Going to school? You what? You got hoofed out of school? HA! HA! What a coincidence. So did I! So did Stubbs as a matter of fact! I got kicked out for jumping off the balcony during an assembly! I didn't really jump off. See, I made a rope out of a bunch of guys' jackets. I was lowering myself down from the balcony so I could sit with my girlfriend.

Teachers wouldn't let us sit together. One of the sleeves ripped. I fell right down, I landed right on top of the teacher who was the Head of the Math Department! Broke his arm! I think that's why they kicked me out. Because of the Head of the Math Department's arm! Glad you're coming with me. I usually try to get a hitchhiker. Gets boring all by myself. Montreal's a good run, though. Only a little over two hours depending on the traffic . . ."

Montreal!

We're thundering out the highway at the speed of light. Doesn't look like there's anywhere he'll have to stop. I've got to tell him now that I don't want to go that far. All I wanted to know was if Dumper Stubbs came out to the grease depot once a week. And now I know. He does. Mr. Fryday was right. Dumper Stubbs is innocent.

What's Rainy Day Delaney going to think when I tell him I want to get out? I could say that I'm going to visit my uncle along the highway here. I'll say, "This is where I get off. I'm going to my uncle's house." Trouble is, there's no houses along Highway 417. O.K. I'll pretend he lives behind the trees over there. That's what I'll say; "I get off here. There's my uncle's house, you can't see it, it's behind those tree over there. He's a hermit."

Rainy Day Delaney is starting to tell all about how his buddy Stubbs got himself kicked out of school for blowing up the science lab and I'm getting ready to tell him I have to get out here in the middle of nowhere.

But now we can't hear anything except a terrible rattling and clanking and banging and knocking. Blue smoke is all around us. The truck is howling and screaming while Rainy Day is cursing and wrestling with the steering wheel and the clutch and the gear shift.

Now we are stopped in a dirty cloud. The truck has died.

I'm glad.

Now I don't have to tell that stupid lie about my uncle the hermit.

I can hitchhike back from here.

Who knows, maybe I'll even be able to catch up with Connie Pan and Dink.

Rainy Day Delaney is on his cellular phone.

He's standing in front of his smoking engine. I'm sitting on the running board deciding what to do. I can hear him on the phone. He's got somebody on the other end. It must be a mechanic. Yes, he'll be here as soon as he can. As a matter of fact, he's not that far. He'll be here in twenty minutes. Then I hear the name. Stubbs! Rainy Day is talking to Dumper Stubbs! He'll be here in a few minutes!

I quickly tell Rainy Day that I've decided to go back to Ottawa and thanks for the ride. Before he gets a chance to say anything I cross the median and get over to the other side of the highway to hitchhike back.

For about fifteen minutes the cars are blowing by so fast I'm thinking I'll never get out of here before Dumper gets here. I don't know why but I just don't want to see him. And I don't want to be standing here when Rainy Day tells him I was asking questions about him. And I don't want to be offered a ride back to the city with him.

A new Chrysler New Yorker with wire wheels stops to pick me up. As I'm running up to get in, a truck pulls up across the highway behind Rainy

Day's truck. I can see writing on the side. STUBBS. But it's not Dumper's truck.

I watch the man get out. I hear his name called by Rainy Day. They are glad to see each other. They are good old friends. They slap each other on the back. They walk around to study the broken truck.

There's only one problem.

One thing not right.

The man who got out of the truck which says STUBBS on the side is a short skinny guy with red hair.

Rainy Day Delaney's friend who he sees once a week at the grease depot is some other guy named Stubbs.

It's not Dumper!

X

They arrest you for riding your bike on the Queensway. They arrest you even worse for riding your bike on the Queensway in the middle of the night. But I'm tearing down the Queensway on my bike.

I'm following Dumper Stubbs's truck west on the Queensway.

He left the Elmdale Tavern and went out Wellington to the corner of Parkdale. I thought he was going to turn right on Parkdale and go down to Westboro Beach. He has a full barrel of grease in the back and I was sure he was going down to the beach to dump it. But no, he turned left, he didn't signal, and went up Parkdale and took the Queensway West ramp.

And I'm following.

Yesterday the Chrysler New Yorker with the wire wheels let me off on Highway 417 at Rideau Road. The guy driving said he was a zipper salesman. He must have been telling the truth because the back of the Chrysler was full of boxes of different kinds of zippers. He was a big fat guy with hair growing out of his nose. He kept telling me all about zippers and fasteners and Velcro and asking me if I had a zipper for the fly of my pants or did I have Velcro or what? Then he told me about how everybody in the world practically had at least one zipper, except maybe some people in some tribe in the bush in New Zealand or somewhere, but think of it, five billion zippers in the world. If he could sell just one zipper to everybody in the world he'd be a billionaire! I was wishing Dink was here to tell him some stuff about the Big Bang Theory or quasars or something to get his mind off zippers and specially get it off *my* zipper!

That's the trouble with hitchhiking. There are so many weirdos driving around.

From there I hitched a ride on a cement truck back to the grease depot.

This guy was even worse. He had a whole lot of naked pictures hanging on his windshield and he kept trying to get me to talk about them. Probably related to that famous hotshot teacher, Mr. Boyle. Then he said he had some more pictures, better ones, films, at home and did I want to go over and check them out.

"Yeah sure," I said. "And I got a friend with a camera, maybe he could come over and take your picture. My friend is six-foot-five and plays defensive end for the Ottawa Rough Riders."

"Hey," this guy said, "you got an attitude son! That mouth of yours could get you in a whole lotta trouble!"

"Let me out of here," I said.

Connie Pan and Dink were gone, of course, and there was nobody around. I grabbed a macaroni and cheese loaf sandwich out of my saddle bag and as I was eating it and getting ready to take off, along came Rainy Day Delaney and the red-headed guy in his truck.

No, Rainy Day definitely never heard of a guy named Dumper Stubbs and nobody by that name ever came out here to the grease depot. But the red-headed guy said he thought he knew Dumper, he's no relative of his though, big ugly guy, sort of a pig, got a wreck of a truck, big steel bumper, picks up grease at restaurants and chipwagons, I think. Doesn't bring it out here though.

Wonder what he does with it?

"He picks up grease at restaurants, too?" I said.

"Yeah," the red-headed guy said, "I've seen him quite a few times at different places, around the back, putting the stuff in his barrel. Big ugly guy. Wears his pants away up around his chest. Got a truck should have been in the junk yard years ago."

"Never laid eyes on the guy," says Rainy Day Delaney. They were packing up some more tools to go back and fix the big truck.

I ate the rest of my sandwiches on my bike on the way back home.

This morning I went to Evangeline Flower Shop on Somerset and bought one red rose. The stem of the rose was almost as long as my arm. It cost $4.50. Evangeline, the beautiful woman who runs the store gave me a little tube of water which she attached to the bottom of the stem. Then she put a piece of feathery green fern with the rose and wrapped it in shiny green paper. Then she said something nice to me in French. I don't know what it was but it was probably something romantic.

I walked down to the Hong Kong Beauty Salon with the rose and looked in the window. Connie Pan was in there, washing a woman's hair. The woman's head was tilted back so far in the sink that it didn't look like part of her. Connie Pan looked up at me and held up one finger. Wait a minute, she meant. It was the same in any language. Hold up one finger. I'll be there in a minute.

Then she came out. Right away I explained to her how I should have told her where we were really going and that it was not a very nice place to go on a picnic, a grease depot. Then I told her how I got sort of trapped in the truck and how I found out about how Dumper Stubbs doesn't deliver the grease out there like he's supposed to. I even told her how I almost told Rainy Day Delaney a lie about my uncle the hermit so he'd stop the truck and let me out.

She laughed at that and then I gave her the rose. She took the rose and put it to her mouth while she sniffed it. With the red rose there she bowed and never moved her eyes off my eyes. Then she went back in and took the woman's head out of the sink and stuck it back on her shoulders.

I walked down to the Mekong Grocery just in time to meet Mr. Fryday carefully parking the chipwagon. He was being very cheerful while he got the burners going and I helped him set out the containers and straighten up the display. And I reminded him, as usual, to switch off his parking lights.

"How was your day off for research, Spud Sweetgrass?" he said very cheerfully. It was so cheerful that it wasn't cheerful at all. He sounded like he was worried about something.

"Research?" I said. I was thinking about the night Dink and I saw him come out of the Elmdale Tavern with Dumper.

"Research on the sign question," said Mr. Fryday, sounding very cheerful.

"Well, Mr. Fryday," I said, "I had a very interesting day of research yesterday. . . ."

I put on Beethoven's Third Symphony, the Second Movement. It's the kind of music that makes you wonder what's going to happen next. It's also sad kind of music. Not sad that makes you cry but sad because you don't know what's going to come next. It's like a funeral of somebody you don't know.

Should I tell him or not?

Like the Second Movement, I didn't know what I was going to say till I said it.

"I looked at many 'open' and 'closed' signs and priced many of the different types, Mr. Fryday, and I came to the conclusion that you don't need *any* signs saying 'OPEN' or 'CLOSED' at all. When a chipwagon is not there, it is closed. When a chipwagon is there, it's open."

This was one of the longest lies I've told all week.

I think Mr. Fryday thought I was being a smart-ass. He scowled at me.

A little while later he left and I got the chips ready for the day.

I played the same Beethoven movement over and over again. In the music, sometimes you know what's going to happen and then all of a sudden you don't. That's why it is very quiet and deep and sad. Something way down deep is rumbling there. Beethoven must have been sad and excited at the same time when he made this music. Dink the Thinker told me Beethoven was deaf. How could you be deaf and make this kind of music?

Just before Mr. Fryday came back for the wagon, along came Connie Pan with a present for me. It was a tiny yellow buttercup, made of silk. She pinned it on my shirt over my heart. I asked her if it was a Vietnamese kind of present to give. She said no. I asked her if it was a Chinese kind of present to give. No, it wasn't. She asked me if the rose I gave her was an Irish kind of present. I didn't know. Was it an Abo kind? I didn't know.

Dink came along and showed us a picture of me getting into a big truck. Then he took our picture. I had my silk buttercup on.

Connie Pan's flower was at home in a long thin vase. When Connie Pan told her mother who gave it to her, her mother scowled at her. Just like Mr. Fryday scowled at me.

The picture shows Connie Pan in the chipwagon and me standing on the sidewalk. Connie Pan is leaning over my shoulder. I am looking at the camera, pointing at the yellow silk buttercup over my heart.

After dark, I went to the Elmdale Tavern and checked out Dumper's truck.

His barrel was full. But not full of grease from Mr. Fryday's fleet of wagons. It's grease from restaurants Dumper's been collecting. How many barrels a week does he collect? How many kitchen sinkfuls of grease does Dumper collect?

And now I'm following, on my bike, Dumper's ugly truck west along the Queensway. It's around midnight and the truck is weaving in and out of the centre lane. I'm sticking to the right lane. I'm hoping Dumper takes an exit soon because the traffic can't see me very well and I feel like I'm going to get killed any minute. I'm as scared as I was that night by my fire when I was nine.

He doesn't take the Island Park exit. He doesn't take the Carling exit. He's pulling away. I'll only make it for one more. If he doesn't take the Maitland exit I'll be too far back. I still see his tail lights. I can tell his tails from the others because the truck's got a broken spring and one side is lower than the other. Also, one light has part of the reflector broken off so it's half red and half white. It looks like I've lost him. He's not signalling. But wait, he's starting to move across two lanes. He's not signalling. I can hear car horns. He's taking the Maitland exit! What a driver! More car horns. He swings right and up the Maitland ramp.

I pump my legs as fast as I can. He has a stop light at the top of the ramp. I'm going top speed as I swing up the ramp. There's three vehicles waiting at the light. Dumper is first. I'm right up behind the third car. The light turns green. Dumper's truck doesn't move. More car horns. Now Dumper moves. He must be half drunk.

Now he swings right and there's more horns because he could have gone a long time ago on the red.

What a driver!

Dumper's not the kind of guy that gets bothered by a horn blowing behind him. I imagine him sitting there while the horns are blowing, his stupid head staring straight ahead.

When somebody blew a horn behind my father, he'd look up into the rear-view mirror and squint his eyes a bit to get a good look at the horn-blower. Then he'd name the note the blower blew.

"F Sharp," he'd maybe say. "But you're flat!"

Dumper crosses the bridge over the Queensway and stops at the next light. All of a sudden, I'm right behind him. I've got nowhere to hide except right under his barrel. He can't see me in either of his side mirrors. I imagine him starting his truck with a jerk and dumping all those kitchen sinkfuls of rancid grease on top of me.

Dumper turns left on Woodward Avenue and then turns into a lot in behind a furniture factory. Around the front of the factory office there's a lawn and a hedge. I throw my bike under the hedge and dive in after it. I crawl along the hedge until I can see Dumper's truck. He's backing it into a parking spot back there.

Dumper sits in his truck for a while. Probably having another booze snooze. Now the door opens and Dumper gets out. He's not too steady on his feet and he's talking to himself. He's trying to get his key into his glove compartment lock. He can't get it in the hole. He waves his hand. Never mind. Now he goes around to the back of the truck and climbs on. It takes him three tries to get on. The first two times he loses his balance and does a little dance around the empty lot for a while. He's up in the truck and even though I crawl out of the hedge a bit, I can't see what he's doing. I can hear a wrench clanking on the barrel. He's turning something. I can hear him gasping and sighing and clearing his throat.

Now he gets down off the truck with something in his hand. Now I can't see him at all.

Next, he comes around the other side of his truck and leans on the door. He turns around and leans in the open window. He takes out a can of beer. He pulls the top. It makes a cracking sound that sounds pretty loud. Shows how quiet it is around here this time of night. In the distance, the Queensway is humming.

Dumper gurgles down half his can of beer and does a big sigh. Then a big long burp that sounds like somebody being strangled.

He sits on the running board and rests his head back on the door. His beer can slowly tilts in his hand. He's dozing off. His head slides sideways across the door a bit and his mouth sags open.

He snores one big snore, like a pig grunting, and the sound wakes him up.

Dumper finishes his beer and clatters the empty can across the paved lot. Then, under his gut, he opens his pants and takes a piss. I can't see but I can hear. This is the longest piss I've ever heard. It goes on and on. It's like somebody left an outside tap on. There. It's over. No, wait, here it comes again. I count to twenty. It stops. Oh, oh! Here comes some more. I can see the reflection of the street light on Woodward Avenue in this lake that Dumper is standing in! Here it comes again! I'm afraid it's going to flow across the lawn and wash me and my bike right out from under the hedge! There can't be any more! There; silence. Whoops, a bit more. One more short one. Now a big sigh.

One more little slurp. Done. Dumper must be up to his ankles in his own piss.

Now he sloshes around to the back of the truck and gets back up in it. I can hear the wrench again against the barrel. But this time the sound is hollow.

Now Dumper gets down from the back of the truck without breaking his neck and walks around and locks the driver's side. Then he staggers out of the lot, right past where I'm lying in the hedge, across the street and down a bit and into the front door of a small apartment building.

Dumper bangs the door open against the wall and disappears inside. I wait for a while to see if a light goes on but it doesn't. Dumper probably lives around the back.

I go over to his truck and check it out. I climb up and tap his barrel with my knuckle. The sound is hollow.

Dumper Stubbs's rancid-grease barrel is empty.

His barrel is the type with a plug in the bottom you can open with a wrench. But there's no grease on the ground. What did he do with it? I pick up a long hose in the truck. It's a type with a screw-on fixture. I lift the hose. It drips grease. I jump down from the truck and check the area again.

I look under the truck. It's too dark to see anything. I crawl carefully under the truck, feeling the pavement with my hands flat. My hands are slapping and splashing in a warm liquid. It's not grease. It smells like . . . It is! It's part of Dumper's lake!

Now I hear a dripping, hollow sound. The echoing sound of Dumper's lake dripping down a well.

Now my hands are on a grate. A thick iron grate with rectangles for holes.

It's a sewer cover.

So that's it.

Dumper runs the grease down a hose from his barrel into a sewer under his truck!

XI

While I'm making my mother a coffee for breakfast I'm thinking.

I'm thinking how Dumper's barrel was full that night Dink and I waited outside the Elmdale and saw him come out with Mr. Fryday. And I'm thinking about how, on the days he'd come around for the trash, I'd hear that dull heavy clunking sound when he'd hit the trash can against the side of the barrel.

A dull, heavy clunking sound, not a hollow sound, means a barrel is full.

And I'm thinking about what the red-headed friend of Rainy Day Delaney said about seeing Dumper collecting grease from restaurants. What if, every day, Dumper collected a full barrel and got paid for collecting a full barrel from the restaurants? And what if he did that every day, six days a week? And another full barrel from Mr. Fryday's wagons on Sundays?

And what if he then, with his wrench and his hose every night . . . ?

And the $15 a barrel he's supposed to pay to the rendering company at the grease depot. Seven barrels times $15 is . . . $105 a week he can steal by just attaching a hose and . . .

Would Dumper break the law, pollute the world, for money?

Suddenly I'm thinking about Dumper Stubbs ruining everybody's beautiful stroll on Sunday in Chinatown just to pick up one cent off the sidewalk.

Sure he would!

While I'm giving my mother her coffee she's combing her short shiny black hair in the mirror. Her eyes move from her own face in the mirror to me. She looks mad.

She tells me that some official phoned from Ottawa Tech and said that if she came over and signed some papers, I could get back into school in the fall. They said this was what always was done when people got kicked out. At Ottawa Tech they're always phoning your place for something. Mostly to try and get you to keep going to school. They must be short of students or something. Maybe it would be better if they had no students at all — then they'd have to fire hot-shot Boyle.

While I'm trying to tell her what happened, about putting my foot on the wall when Boyle came along and how Connie Pan was there, she keeps saying that everything's falling apart because my father's dead and then we start having a big fight.

She's yelling how my father got laid off at the paper mill for mouthing off and how I'm doing the same now and mouthing off and now I get mean and I say why is she hanging around across the street at the Village Inn so much and I'm not the only one falling apart. And then I tell her I'm going to get hot-shot Boyle for this, it's all his fault.

Maybe I'll get a big sign that says *Boyle has lunch with naked ladies at Valentino's all the time!* and carry it up and down Albert Street in front of Ottawa Tech!.

All this in the mirror!

But now she looks away from the mirror and looks at me straight on.

And now I've never seen my mother's beautiful face so sad.

"Oh my God, John!" she cries. "Oh John, I'm so, so sorry," she cries. Now she's looking past me. For a minute I think she's speaking to my father! I look over my shoulder to see if he's standing there.

"Why are you so sorry?" I say. "What are you sorry about?"

"It was so selfish of me," she cries. "I never thought of it until now. It never entered my head until just this instant," she cries, her face sort of falling apart, tears spilling out of her eyes.

She puts her strong thin arms around me and squeezes me.

"What do you mean?" I say. "What are you talking about?"

"I didn't see it till now," she says in my ear, her wet cheek on my cheek, "that you miss him just as much as I do. That you loved him just as much as I did. That you lost him, too!"

She pushes me away from her so she can hold me with her eyes.

"I was behaving," she says, "I've been acting as though I'm the only mourner around here, the only one who lost everything."

She squeezes my shoulders.

"My God, John! I forgot all about you all this time!"

Now she's got me crying.

"It must have been so lonesome for you, these past months. I'm so, so sorry," she says softly.

Now I'm telling her everything, just like I used to. All about hot-shot Boyle and being kicked out of school and about Dumper Stubbs and the poisoned beach and about Connie Pan and E.S.L. volleyball . . .

"I'll have a little chat with hot-shot Boyle for starters," my mother says, and when she says that, I can feel muscles in her voice.

"That Connie Pan, she sounds nice," she says, "why don't you bring her over some time? I think I might know her mother. She comes into the Resource Centre. She's a community leader. If you're not Chinese she'll call you Bignose!"

"That's her!" I say. "That's the one!"

"Don't be too sure," she says. "A lot of the new Chinese Canadians say that. They don't mean any harm, they're just scared. You think what it would be like to live in China, not speaking the language hardly at all, surrounded by people with little noses and different shaped eyes. It wouldn't be easy. Connie doesn't say that though, eh?"

"No, she just laughs at it."

"At what, your nose?" my mother says, doing one of her old jokes.

Then, as she drinks a drink of her coffee, and looks over her cup at me, I see the green flecks flashing in her brown eyes.

I give Dink a call and tell him to meet me at the chipwagon as soon as he can.

At work, Mr. Fryday doesn't even mention my research on the "open" and "closed" business. He's being his cheerful old self, praising me up for being

94

a good businessman and selling those chips like hot cakes and putting on just the right Beethoven music to get the customers in the right mood. He hangs around polishing his rings and talking to some people passing by until he can give the old taste test to the first potato chip. Surprise! He doesn't even tell me that I should have left it in a few more seconds or that I should have taken it out a couple of seconds earlier.

"Just right, Spud Sweetgrass!" says Mr. Fryday.

Under his arm he's got today's *Ottawa Citizen*. He's reading a story in the local section while he's tasting his perfect Beethoven's chip. He's singing softly his "My day is Fryday" song and flashing his rings and gold tooth in the sun's rays. Then he leaves the paper open on the counter, open at the story he's been reading in the local section, so I'll read it.

"Beach Re-opens" the headline says. Then it tells all about how the mighty Ottawa River has washed away all the pollution from Westboro Beach and the water's been tested and the authorities at Regional Environment have given the beach the O.K. for swimming again. Then it gives stuff about how many times the beach was closed last year and how many swimmers used the beach this year and all that.

No wonder Mr. Fryday's in such a good mood. No more grease being dumped on the beach, eh Mr. Fryday? No more pollution? Your buddy Stubbs is off the hook. It's all over. Let's pretend it never happened. You can relax now. Back to business as usual.

Sure.

While I'm waiting for Dink to get here and working out my plan along comes Connie Pan and, oh, oh, she's with her mother. They're not walking like they're going to walk by, either. They're walking like they're walking to see me!

I have to watch my mouth.

I'm smiling to myself, thinking of how my mother knows Connie's mother.

Up they come. Connie Pan looks at me and shrugs her shoulders. I'm wearing my silk buttercup. She looks at it and smiles.

Mrs. Pan starts right in. Connie Pan rolls her eyes.

"Why give rose to my daughter?" says Mrs. Pan.

I can see she's looking at my nose. She's so far down there on the sidewalk and I'm so far up here, my nose must be hanging down like an elephant's trunk. I make up a quick order of fries.

"Why give rose, Bignose?" she says.

I give the fries to her.

"Rose is a gift. Like chips. I give you chips — a gift," I say. I know it's stupid to talk bad broken English to people who can't speak English very well but I guess I can't help it because I always do it. Except with Connie Pan. I don't do it with her.

She takes the fries. Connie Pan tries one.

I turn up Beethoven's Third Symphony, Third Movement which is now playing. At least it's happier than the second movement.

"Why go on dirty road?" says Mrs. Pan.

Why do Chinese daughters tell their mothers everything? Maybe it's a Chinese tradition. Tell your mother everything.

"We were going on a picnic and I took the wrong road," I say. Canadian sons tell their mothers lies. And their girlfriend's mothers too. It's a Canadian tradition.

"Not bike no more on dirty road!" says Mrs. Pan, wagging her finger.

"No, Mrs. Pan, I promise. No more on dirty road bike," I say, being a bit of smart ass.

"O.K.," she says. Then she takes another look at my nose and turns and walks away. Connie Pan goes with her. After a few steps, Connie Pan does this amazing thing. She turns her head to me and kisses the air!

I feel my face get deep red and hot. When I stop watching her walk up Somerset Street with her mother and when my face cools off I see Dink the Thinker there in front of me, taking my picture from the step of the Mekong Grocery.

"Nice flower," says Dink, his camera in front of his face.

"Flower is gift," I say. "Like chips. I give you chips—a gift." I give Dink a free order of fries. He douses them with vinegar and salt and then we look at my picture. Pretty good picture of an elephant wearing a silk buttercup over his heart.

In between customers I tell Dink everything. When I get to the part about Dumper's lake he can hardly control himself, he's so excited. Then I tell about the hose and the sewer grate.

All of a sudden we both get the same great idea at the same time!

The camera!

We have a good solid big supper at Dink's place because we've got a lot of biking to do. We get a whole load of take-out from the Chu Ching Restaurant next door to the Hong Kong Beauty Salon after Mr. Fryday gives us a big happy goodbye and

97

drives off carefully in his truck. I pay for the take-out because today's payday and because Dink has no money because he spent it all on a flash for his camera.

We have spring rolls, shrimp fried rice, moo koo guy pan, shrimp chop suey, vegetable chow mein, bar-b-q pork almond diced, moo koo har kew, mushroom egg foo young and almond cookies.

Even Dink's dad has a taste of a few dishes in between cigarettes. But when he coughs a whole lot of chop suey all over the wall, he leaves the kitchen and goes to bed.

We watch TV for a while to kill some time and let the take-out food go down a bit. We watch a show that Dink wants to see about a quasar they just found as big as our whole solar system. It gives off a light brighter than 1,000 galaxies of 100 billion stars each, the astronomer on TV tells us. Dink always plays his science shows really loud so his dad can hear them in the other room. "That's a lotta light!" Dink's dad shouts and then coughs through the rest of the program.

At about ten o'clock we ride down Somerset to Wellington and the Elmdale Tavern to check out Dumper's truck. It's there alright, and he's got a full barrel of grease in the back. I check his glove compartment. It's still locked.

We get back on our bikes and ride west on Wellington until it changes into Richmond Road. We're not taking the Queensway to Dumper's place. This way is safer. And longer. And slower. But we're not in a hurry. We'll be there before Dumper gets there.

We cross the Queensway at Maitland and turn up Woodward.

We hide our bikes under the hedge and walk across the dark lot to where Dumper's parking spot is.

We stand over the sewer grate where Dumper Stubbs will put his hose down. I stand beside the grate and point at it. Dink flashes my picture. We go back to the hedge and lie down near our bikes and check out the picture with my pen flashlight. The picture is perfect. Dink's flash works great.

I can see Dink's eyes are pretty wide.

He can't wait to catch this criminal in the act with his instant camera.

We go back out to the sewer. This time I take Dink's picture standing beside the grate. This time, Dink's not pointing. He's standing with his arms folded and his foot on the grate, like an old-fashioned picture of a guy who just shot a lion.

Back at the hedge, there's a big man standing with his foot on our bikes, like a guy in an old-fashioned picture who just shot two lions. There's a light on now in the front window of the furniture factory.

"What the hell are you kids doing here?" says the guy. "Get away from that truck." He's got sawdust in the hair on his arms. He's wearing a belt with a tape measure attached and he's got a hammer in a holster on the side. He must be from inside the furniture factory.

"Just trying out this new camera we got for our birthday," I say. "My brother and me, we're twins, we got this summer school project, in night photography," I say, telling the longest lie of my career so far.

"Well, you can't hang around here, this is private property. Get the hell out of here," says the guy, and gives our bikes a kick.

We walk our bikes out of the lot and down Woodward Avenue till we're out of sight of the furniture factory hedge. We hide our bikes behind a pile of fresh sod and slide back in the shadows behind the factory.

"Twins?" says Dink. "I should have got a picture of that lie!"

There's some lights coming into the lot.

It's Dumper's truck.

He turns and backs into his spot. He's over his sewer grate.

We're sitting in the bushes right behind his truck. If it was daylight, he'd see us sitting there, just like two crows on a fence. But in the dark, if we don't move, he won't. His broken tail light lights us up like a searchlight. But that light will be out when he comes around the back of the truck to put down his hose.

Out comes Dumper, grunting and talking to himself.

I've got my hand on Dink. I don't want him to move until exactly the right time. Dumper's going to see the flash. So we've only got one shot. Dumper climbs up on his truck. He gets his hose and his wrench. He turns the plug at the bottom of the barrel with the wrench, takes out the plug, jams the plug end of the hose into the hole, tightens the hose. You can hear gurgling. Here comes the grease. Dumper gets down off the truck. He doesn't look as drunk tonight, not like he was last night.

He's down off the truck without staggering. He's puffing a bit, though. He's got the end of the hose in his hand. It's spouting grease. You can hear the grease splashing on the pavement.

He leans under the truck with the dangling hose. He tries a couple of times and then finds the grate. Finds one of the rectangle holes.

He's on his knees. He's placing the flowing hose.

I let go of Dink's arm.

Dink flashes the picture. Gotcha!

Dumper lifts up and bangs his head under his truck so hard that he goes back down. His head hitting the truck sounds like the dull heavy clunking sound of something hollow hitting something full. I guess the something hollow part is Dumper's head.

Now Dumper's mad. He crawls out from under the truck and charges right at us. He's blind from the flash and so are we. He's so fast crawling, he's like an animal, a bear maybe. He's growling and cursing. Dink and I are moving away from the back of the truck. There's bushes blocking our way a bit. The other way is easier. Dumper is crawling and grunting and swearing. Dink trips over a cinder block along the edge and his camera flies ahead along the pavement. Now Dink is crawling. Dink and Dumper are both crawling towards the camera. I jump over Dink and kick the camera ahead so Dumper won't get it. I run and kick it again. Then I lean over and pick it up. I run towards Woodward Avenue and our bikes. Dink is running now too. We can't see but we can sort of see. Dumper's tangled up in his grease hose. He's slipping around in the cooking grease, the hose whipping around his feet. He falls on his back.

I'm at the bikes where we hid them. I can hear the carpenter yelling from the furniture factory about what's going on out there. I'm on my bike. Dink's got his bike. I've got the camera. We take off down Woodward Avenue the other way to Clyde Avenue. We cut up Clyde to Carling. We stop at Churchill and Carling to get our breath. There's nobody following us. We pull in behind Hakim Optical and sit on the grass there.

Dink is puffing and snorting and almost crying. The knees of his pants are ripped and his elbows are bleeding.

I give him his camera. There are pieces hanging off it. He tries to eject the developed picture. It's jammed. The track is broken. The camera is smashed.

Dink looks up at me.

He shakes his head.

We haven't got a camera anymore.

We haven't got the picture either.

In fact, we haven't got anything except torn pants and bleeding elbows.

XII

Twelve little kids tied together with a rope. Their keeper is a girl with shorts on and hiking boots. The kids are driving her crazy. She has a stick that she uses to keep the kids from walking off the sidewalk. They're lined up at my wagon. Their keeper is trying to figure out their orders.

Every kid wants something different. One wants a small order with vinegar in the middle and no salt. The next one wants a medium with salt in the middle and no vinegar. The next one wants a large to split with his friend but he wants salt and vinegar and his friend is not allowed to have salt or vinegar because his doctor said. Another kid wants a small order with salt and vinegar on the bottom, salt in the middle and vinegar on top. The next kid wants only half a small order with no salt and no vinegar but is there any ketchup? Another kid is sulking because there's no Pogo Sticks.

Now the keeper wants to know about the calories in each chip. She's on a diet. What kind of fat do I use? Is there cholesterol?

Now the kid who wanted a small order with vinegar in the middle and no salt changes his mind. Now he wants a medium order to go halves with his buddy and now they're arguing about ketchup even though I've told them about fifteen times that there is no ketchup! Now the keeper is telling them that's it, they're only allowed small orders so the ones who ordered medium and large have to order again, start figuring it out all over again.

Now, because these kids are changing their orders, some of the other kids decide they'll change their minds too and we're all almost back where we started.

All the time I'm trying to decide if I'm going to tell Mr. Fryday about what Dink and I know about Dumper Stubbs. I'm also wondering what Dink is finding out at the Regional Environment Office. Dink is doing research. It's two days since his camera got smashed. He's already got a new camera from the warranty. These cameras are supposed to be unbreakable under normal use.

Is kicking your camera around the pavement to keep it away from a crazy man normal use? I guess so.

Dink has also read two books on grease already. Used cooking grease gets re-cycled and is used to make soap, pig food and lipstick. Lipstick! My mom wears lipstick. I wonder if I should tell her what it's made from. Hey, Mom, that stuff you're putting on your mouth? It used to be in a barrel in the back of Dumper Stubbs's truck! Hey, Mom, when you put on more lipstick, what happened to the lipstick you put on before? You what? You licked it off and you swallowed it? Gross!

She'll laugh at that.

I look at the keeper. She's wiping her lips with a serviette. The kids are tangled up in their rope and fighting and dumping chips on the sidewalk and squirting vinegar on each other. The keeper uses the side mirror of the truck and takes out a tube of lipstick. She smears it on her upper lip first, then she stretches her lower lip flat and drags a thick layer of lipstick on there. Then she presses her lips together and fixes her hair a bit. The lipstick she had on before. What happened to it? Did she kiss all these little kids and use it all up that way? I don't think so. I think she hates these little kids.

"What happened to the lipstick you had on before?" I say to her. I'm feeling very sarcastic. My mouth is going to get me in trouble, I can feel it.

"Pardon?" says the keeper.

"What happened to all the lipstick you had on before?"

"What do you mean?"

"Didn't you have lipstick on this morning or an hour ago or something? What happened to it? I mean, how come you have to put more on? Where does it go? Where does lipstick go?"

"What are you, a smart ass?" says the keeper.

"Do you know what lipstick's made of?" I say. "Do you know it's made from re-cycled rancid grease from chipwagons? And you probably licked it all off and swallowed it. How many times a day do you put that stuff on anyway. About ten times a day?"

"None of your business, you creep! What do I owe you for this mess?"

"Let's see, thirteen small orders of fries will be $19.50. Would you like a small cup of grease to go? No extra charge. Take it along with you?

Where's the next stop for your act? Do your little animals do any other tricks?"

All of a sudden I hear Mr. Fryday's voice coming from around behind the truck where the propane tanks are strapped on.

"Put your money away madam. These chips are on the house. On the wagon, I should say. No, no, I insist. There is absolutely no reason that you should be treated with such rudeness. I apologize on behalf of my employee here. My, what cute kids! Day camp is it? You're doing a wonderful job. Think nothing of it. My name is Fryday. Everyday is Fryday as they say. Have a nice day! Goodbye."

I have a feeling I'm going to be fired. It's the same feeling I had just before I got kicked out of school. Well, if he's going to be mad at me and maybe fire me, he might as well be good and mad at me. I'll tell him about Dumper.

I'll tell him right now, before he starts this speech that he is just going to start.

"Mr. Fryday, the other night I followed Dumper Stubbs home and I watched him pour a whole barrel of cooking oil down into the sewer where he parks his truck. Here's a picture I had taken."

I show Mr. Fryday the picture of me standing, pointing at the sewer grate.

"And I went out to the grease depot where you say he takes the stuff. They never heard of him. Those receipts he gives you must be forgeries. My friend Dink and I are going to prove he's doing it and report him!"

Mr. Fryday's face is a storm.

For a long time he stares at the picture. A picture of a kid pointing at a sewer. What does that prove?

"We got a picture of him doing it but it didn't turn out," I say.

Then for a long time Mr. Fryday looks at me. Then he rips the picture in half. Then in half again.

Then he speaks.

"You're just like your father. You Abos are all the same. Making stuff up about pollution. Your father was kicked out of his job at the paper plant across the river for the same thing! When will you ever learn?"

He looks at me, shaking his head.

"Get out of my chipwagon, Spud Sweetgrass," he says quietly.

Beethoven's Seventh Symphony, the Second Movement, the Allegretto, is playing in the background while Mr. Fryday fires me.

Beethoven's Seventh Symphony, Second Movement, is perfect music when you're getting fired.

As I'm walking down Rochester Street, Dink catches up to me. He's so excited he can hardly talk. Under his arm is a long roll of paper. He's also carrying books and pamphlets and charts and photographs. He's telling me all about all this stuff he got from the Department of Physical Environment.

We go into my place and spread the big roll of paper out on the floor.

I put one corner of the huge map under a chair leg. Dink and I lean on the other two corners of the map while we're studying it and talking. There's only one corner of the map left to hold down.

My mother stands on it for us.

It's a map of all the sewers in Ottawa. There's two kinds of sewers. Sanitary sewers and storm sewers. The sanitary sewers are shown by a solid line. The storm sewers are marked with a broken line. Little arrows show what direction the sewers flow in.

While we're doing this I tell my mother how Mr. Fryday fired me and why.

"It figures," she says. "The man is threatened somehow. You must be on to something."

With a yellow highlighter, we trace along the broken line from the "catch basin" on Woodward Avenue where Dumper parks his truck. The line goes along for a few blocks then under the Queensway, down Broadview, a few more blocks, across Carling to Tilbury, eight blocks along Tilbury to Wavell, four blocks down Wavell, across Richmond Road, under the Parkway and out into the Ottawa River.

Not far down the river from that pipe outlet is a bay. And guess what? Right! Westboro Beach is in that bay.

The grease from Dumper's barrels travels about twenty blocks under the city, out the seventy-two-inch pipe at the end of Wavell, then slides down river to get caught in the bay. And to poison the beach.

But there's something Dink and I can't figure out. Where is all this grease right now? How come the beach is open? Is the grease caught somewhere?

It says on this map that the pipe at the Wavell outlet is seventy-two inches. That's a big pipe.

I double ride Dink over to his place to get his bike. We ride to the Wavell outlet.

The pipe there is as high as I am. There's water running out of it. I dip my finger in the stream of water running out of the high pipe into the river. It doesn't feel greasy. In fact the water doesn't even seem dirty. It doesn't even smell bad. Is our map wrong? There's an iron gate covering the opening of the pipe. The gate is locked with a padlock. No Ninja Turtle games please. We pull on the gate but it's solid. No sewer walking for Dink and me today.

I tell Dink that we've got to find out where all this grease is.

We get back on our bikes and ride to the corner of Holland and Wellington to the offices in Holland Cross where Dink got the map and the other stuff.

Inside, on the wall, is a huge framed-in-glass copy of the map that Dink and I have at home. I run my finger up and across the glass, tracing the route of Dumper's grease.

Behind us, a voice.

"Can I help you boys?"

I explain.

"We know a guy who dumps a barrel of used cooking grease down a catch basin every night. We know it pollutes Westboro Beach but we can't prove it."

This is a man who is so tall that he has to duck when he takes us into his office. He has a pile of bushy grey hair and his eyebrows are also grey and they move around like giant fuzzy caterpillars when he talks. His hands are as big as baseball gloves and his ears are big and pasted on like Spock's.

I tell him everything.

His eyebrows are going crazy when he says, "This is a very serious charge."

He specially wants to know if we know where the substance is kept each day before it is illegally dumped.

Yes, we do. In the back of a truck outside the Elmdale Tavern.

He shuts his office door.

He says he's not supposed to do what he's going to do. He seems excited, like a little kid. Dink and I are looking at each other. We're both thinking that it's funny, watching a big guy like this squirming around, being excited like a little kid.

He goes into a cupboard and pulls out a box. He takes out of the box a plastic pill that looks like a cod liver oil pill only about three times as big. The liquid inside is clear, like water.

"Don't tell *anyone* about this. This is a dye capsule. You drop one of these in your man's barrel every night before he goes home to dump. One capsule per barrel. That's all you have to do. Wait till it's dark. Don't get caught, don't take any chances. Don't tell anybody. Just walk by the truck and flip the capsule into the barrel. Has the barrel got a lid? No. Good. Just walk casually by, whistle or something, minding your own business, and flip one of these babies into his barrel. This will dissolve and it will mark the grease and everything the grease touches. This is a tracer dye. It will be red. Your man's river of rancid grease will be red! Do this every night."

He was pretty excited, making a flipping move, like he was flipping a coin, when he told us to flip the capsule into the barrel.

"Why doesn't the grease come out the pipe?" I say. "Like it did before?"

"We'll have to wait for that," he says. "We have to wait for Mother Nature," he says.

"Mother Nature?" says Dink.

He takes us out of his office to the map on the wall. I trace my finger over the glass for him, showing him the route the grease is supposed to be taking.

"Perfect," says our man. "Your grease will come pouring out that Wavell outlet, bright red, red as blood. And then we'll charge him!"

Dink and I are still waiting.

"But in the meantime," he says, looking around like he's telling us a secret, "meantime we'll have to pray."

"Pray?"

"Pray! Pray for rain! You need a nice, big rain storm to make it happen. We had a good one a couple of weeks ago. That's why your beach was closed. That grease is heavy. All that grease is just waiting there to be flushed out. We need a nice big storm. Then, bang!, we've got him! But God will have to flush the toilet for us first."

There's an idea that my father would like. Praying for rain.

To God, or the great Spirit of the Abos!

XIII

Mr. Fryday just phoned.

I'm "unfired"!

On the phone he tells me he wants to see me right away, this morning, and that everything's O.K. and not to worry and that I'm not fired anymore.

That's what I say to my mother as she's rushing out the door, late for work.

"Hey, Mom," I shout, "I just got unfired!"

She stops at the door and looks at me, her head tilted a bit, a little smile.

"You're a chip off the old block, you know that? And I think you're even going to be handsomer than he was."

I say goodbye to her.

As she's going down the stairs she calls out: "Be careful, John! There's something serious going on!"

"Don't worry," I say, "I will."

I can't wait to tell Dink that Mr. Fryday wants to "unfire" me.

"UN-fire you?" he'll say. "No such word."

Every night all week long Dink and I walked casually by Dumper's truck outside the Elmdale

Tavern, minding our own business, even whistling sometimes just for a laugh, and flipped one of those babies into Dumper's barrel, just like our eyebrow man said. And we dreamed of a red river of rancid grease.

And I dream of nailing Dumper Stubbs.

I go down the backstairs and jump on my bike and race down and over to Bayswater Avenue. Mr. and Mrs. Fryday are having breakfast on the verandah.

Above, the clouds are racing like a herd of caribou across the sky.

Mr. Fryday is his old self, smiling and praising and glittering. Mrs. Fryday just stares straight ahead, nibbling at her little pieces of toast and jam that Mr. Fryday has so carefully cut on her plate for her. After Mr. Fryday gets me a lemonade and a doughnut he starts praising me up and telling Mrs. Fryday what an intelligent young man I am and how nice my mother is and how glad he is that I am going back to school and how, after I graduated from school how I will be a big success and how he knew my father and loved to hear him play the trombone and how proud my father would be of his big handsome son with all the good ideas about business and especially how his son is not afraid to speak his mind, stand up to authority when he sees something wrong, even though he might put his job in danger . . .

There is a whole lot more in his speech but I can't hear it now because my father is on the stage, playing his solo at the Penguin Club, playing his solo in the piece he wrote, "Hanging Gardens," with Nebuchadnezzar and the Babylonians' Jazz and Swing Band.

And everybody is up cheering.

". . . courage of his convictions," Mr. Fryday is telling Mrs. Fryday. "Now, Spud Sweetgrass, I must tell you that you were right about Angelo."

"Stubbs?" I say.

"Yes, you were right about what Angelo Stubbs was doing with the grease. And you were right about the faked receipts. He had a whole pad of blank receipts locked in the glove compartment of his truck. I went out to the grease depot and you were right, they had never met him. I was very ashamed. I confronted Angelo, you see Angelo is my brother-in-law and I've tried to do my best for him because I promised Mrs. Fryday here, didn't I dear? I promised Mrs. Fryday that I would take care of her brother as much as I could. He's always been a problem, you see, suffered brain damage as a child. Was hit on the head with a snowball with a rock inside it. However, when I looked into your accusations, Spud, and found them to be accurate, I confronted my brother-in-law and he confessed the whole thing. I immediately took him off the grease detail. He now no longer picks up spent cooking grease from Fryday's Classical Chipwagons. He still does the trash and his truck is still available for maintenance, but this irresponsible act of pouring grease down the sewer and having it end up in the river is at an end, thanks to you, Spud Sweetgrass. Now, I formally reinstate you as a valued employee on Mr. Fryday's team. What do you say? Will you rejoin my firm? Let bygones be bygones? And please accept this cheque as a bonus, for having the courage of your convictions. It's a cheque for a full week's vacation with pay. So, you see, you've never been away, have you? Your father would be so proud!"

So that's why he was with him that night in the Elmdale Tavern. Dumper is his brother-in-law and he's taking care of him to do his poor wife a favour!

Should I tell him about the other six barrels a week? About the capsules? About the red rancid river that's coming?

"Who picks up your grease now?" I ask.

"Our grease, Spud, our grease!"

"Our grease. Who picks up our grease now?"

"Oh, a reputable firm. The grease question is no longer in our hands. It's a headache we're well rid of, don't you think? And, by the way, I would be careful how I talk to Angelo for a while, because he knows that you are the one who discovered this unfortunate activity and reported it to me and he is quite angry at you. But it will pass. I have convinced Angelo that you have done him and all of us a very great favour. Imagine, if this had gotten out of hand and the authorities became involved? There are heavy fines and even possible jail sentences for such activity. You are our hero, Spud Sweetgrass!"

Sure. A hero. I bet Dumper thinks I'm a hero. I bet Dumper would like to kill me. I bet Dumper dreams of boiling me in rancid fat. Shipping me to Montreal in a drum of rotten lard.

Should I tell Mr. Fryday about what's really going on? About the other six barrels a week?

I'll tell him later, maybe.

I'll see what happens.

Mr. Fryday's not part of it now, anyway.

And I don't want to warn Dumper. If I tell Mr. Fryday, he'll fire me again, or he'll tell Dumper and Dumper will get away.

No, I won't tell him.

I take the bonus cheque, fold it, and put it carefully in my shirt pocket, just under my silk buttercup. I give the pocket a pat.

"Excellent!" says Mr. Fryday. "Isn't this excellent, dear?" he says to his wife. His wife nods a little but doesn't look at him. I don't think she understands.

"Have some more lemonade, Spud Sweetgrass! What a beautiful name! Sweetgrass!"

Mr. Fryday doesn't know it but he's just said a word that could put his brother-in-law in jail. Sweetgrass.

"I won't be able to start until tomorrow," I tell him, as I gulp down the lemonade.

"Fine, Spud Sweetgrass," he says, and we wave goodbye.

XIV

It's Connie Pan's day off from work and she and Dink and me, we're off to meet Nenaposh the Medicine Man. He's an old man who was a friend of my father's. He loved my father and I remember us visiting him over on Britannia Road when I was a little kid. He told me at my father's funeral if there was anything I needed or I was in trouble or anything to call him on the phone. He gave me his phone number and told me not to tell anybody what it was.

A few days ago I phoned him and explained everything to him about Dumper and the grease, the whole works. There was a long long quiet at the other end of the phone. Then Nenaposh spoke very slowly and seriously.

"Come to my place tomorrow and bring some tobacco with you. It must be tobacco that is not associated with metal or coins in any way. In other words, you cannot buy the tobacco. It must be given to you or you must get it somehow. I will get a holy man I know to bless it. This you needn't know anything about. Don't knock on my door. Leave the tobacco on my step. Three days later, for

I must fast for three days, I will meet you at twelve o'clock noon, when the sun is high and strong. I will meet you and your friends at Kitchissippi Lookout. There, you will be my assistants. Also, at that time, one of your friends must present to me a gift, a simple gift, wrapped in a plain piece of cloth, and tied with red yarn. The gift must be priceless but simple."

Dink and I got a full ashtray off his dad's bureau and we broke open all the butts and collected a whole handful of tobacco. I took it over in a jar and left it on Nenaposh's step. Then I went and discussed with Connie Pan what a "priceless" gift would be. We thought for a long time about diamonds and jewels and other "priceless" things. Then I told her that old Nenaposh said a "simple" priceless gift. Then Connie Pan said that she always thought "priceless" in English was the same as "worthless." Something with no price on it.

We went out in her back yard on Cambridge Street and picked the top off a big thistle. The top of a thistle isn't worth anything. Connie Pan is right. You can't sell it to anybody for anything. It has no price. It is priceless. A priceless purple flower with thorns around. Connie Pan wrapped it in a piece of plain cloth and tied it with red yarn.

We are at Kitchissippi Lookout, Dink and Connie Pan and me.

Down on Westboro Beach is my medicine Man, building a fire on the sand. There is a big crowd of beach freaks standing around. Connie Pan's E.S.L. volleyball players are there.

Nenaposh, the Medicine Man, lights the fire. Nenaposh has reddish skin and black eyes. He has a long black braid hanging. He has one tooth sticking over his lip.

He opens his suitcase beside the fire. He takes out a blanket with patterns of birds and fish and beaver on it. He places a small blue cloth in the middle of the blanket.

He removes all metal from his body, coins from his pocket, his knife, his belt, his watch, his pen from his shirt pocket and places these things on the sand away from the blanket. Out of his suitcase he takes his medicine bag. It is light brown and is made of soft moose hide. From the bag he takes a pipe which is in two pieces. He puts the pipe on the blue cloth. He looks up at the sky. He moves the pipe over a little bit.

He takes an eagle feather from his medicine bag and places it with the quill end almost touching the pipe. He takes out a cup from the bag and sends Dink to the river to fill it up with Ottawa River water. He places the cup of Ottawa River water on the other side of the blue cloth.

He takes some long dry sweetgrass from his bag and places it just exactly right on the cloth.

He looks up at the sky. He moves the cup a little closer to the sweetgrass. He takes a wooden bowl out of his bag and places it on the cloth under the eagle feather. He takes Connie Pan's priceless gift and places it. He places the tobacco I left for him on his step. He takes out some cedar boughs, some sage, a stone, a seashell and some roots and places them.

Then he puts the empty medicine bag on the cloth right exactly where it should go.

In the wooden bowl he places some tobacco and breaks up some pieces of cedar bough, some sage and some sweetgrass. He reaches in the fire and pulls out a burning stick.

He lights the sweetgrass, sage, cedar bough and tobacco in the bowl.

He brings Connie Pan and Dink and me closer. He scoops the smoke from the bowl up into our faces with his hands. Then our hair. Then the front of our clothes and our hands. He scoops the smoke with his hands up to his own face and waves his long black braid in it.

When the fire in the bowl is finished, he digs a hole and buries the ashes in the sand.

Now he picks up the pipe and fills it with tobacco. He lights the pipe with another burning stick. He begins to talk and smokes the pipe and points it this way and then the opposite way. East for the Yellow People. North for the White People, west for the Red People, south for the Black People. Then he names all animals from worms to eagles. And all growing things from grains of wheat to great oak trees. Then points the pipe to the water. Then to the sun. Then specially he points to the women and then to the men and then very specially to the children on Westboro Beach.

Now he passes the pipe around to the left, right around the fire. If you don't want to smoke it, you just rub the middle of it. While the pipe is going around, Nenaposh the Medicine Man takes out a whistle made of the bone of an animal and blows on it and begins to sing "Hé Hé Hé Hé" very quietly and begins to dance very softly without lifting his feet off the sand. And he says words that we don't understand.

And some words we do understand: the wild rice at the edge of the water, the syrup from the maple tree, the berry on the bush, the moose in the wood, the beaver in the pond, the balsam gum to heal . . . the balsam boughs you cut with your own knife to make a shelter alone beside a lake when your father was only ten minutes away.

I'm half in a trance listening to Nenaposh quietly singing "Hé Hé Hé Hé" and dancing softly and blowing on his bone whistle. The Pham family are swaying back and forward with the rhythm and sort of dancing without lifting their feet. The beach freaks are lying around looking at us over their sunglasses or under their sunglasses and lying on their stomachs with their chins on their hands watching, their knees bent, the bottoms of their feet getting a suntan. Or they are lying on their sides, on their elbows while the little kids are kicking sand, trying to dance to Nenaposh's rain dance rhythm.

If only my father and his trombone were here!

Is it the trance I'm in, or is it my imagination? Do I hear howling, and do I see, out the corner of my eye, flashing lightning? Is the Medicine Man's Rain Dance working already?

No, it's not.

It's the cops!

What I'm actually hearing is sirens and what I'm actually seeing when I turn around is two cop cars pulling up and three cops getting out. The pipe is passed to Nenaposh. He breaks it back into two pieces. He kicks the fire out. The volleyball team helps him.

"O.K.," says Nenaposh, "the ceremony is over! The medicine will work. Hello, officers, you're right on time. My friends and I have just put out a very dangerous fire. I think somebody was trying to burn down your lovely sand beach!"

While the cops are writing down all our names, Nenaposh the Medicine Man carefully puts all his medicine back in the medicine bag and puts the bag and the cloth and the blanket in his suitcase.

After I'm finished explaining to one of the cops that my name is Sweetgrass, not Snotgrass, I look around for Nenaposh. I run up to Kitchissippi Lookout and look up and down the Ottawa River Parkway.

There is no sign of the Medicine Man.

The cops are still down around the fire. They're sniffing the ashes of the fire. The kids told them something was buried. They're digging around, looking for what was buried. Looking for what Nenaposh gave back to the earth.

You can tell by the way they act, these cops don't like Nenaposh.

Well, that's just too bad.

They're too late. His spell is already cast! Now we wait for the rain. The sky is moving around like soup just before it starts to boil.

What did Nenaposh say to me, as the cops were coming down the beach? Oh, yes. "You're gonna have rain within twelve hours. I put some extra medicine in, so it's gonna be big! I put in extra because your father played such sweet trombone. If I was you, I'd go home and shut the windows. This is gonna be a big one!"

Now, the clouds are already racing across the sky like herds of elk running from a helicopter!

XV

We sit around on the benches at Kitchissippi Lookout and look at Dink's pictures of Nenaposh the Medicine Man's Rain Dance. Down on Westboro Beach the beach freaks and the E.S.L. volleyballers and mothers and the fathers and the uncles and the kids are starting to look around and talk about going home. They point over at the sky getting black. A big purple wolf is coming out of the west. It is chasing the little white sheep above us. A wind like a wild kitten runs around Westboro Beach. Sand starts lifting in the air. Clothes and plastic cups, towels and lunches, books, socks, sunglasses, parts of castles, little pails and shovels, blankets, Kleenex, bottles of sun-shield are chasing each other up and down.

Connie Pan and Dink and me, we get on our bikes and ride home, dirt blowing in our eyes. Outside Connie Pan's house I say goodbye to her. While we're saying goodbye, the rain falls out of the black monster above us. I can see Mrs. Pan shutting the windows. I wave at her. She doesn't wave back.

By the time I get my bike into the back shed at 179D Rochester Street, there's hail bouncing all over the place like there's an explosion in a ping-pong ball factory someplace nearby in Chinatown.

This is a better storm than the last one even!

I go in and call the Department of Physical Environment, the special number the eyebrow man gave me. He tells me that if this storm lasts through the night it will be enough to drive the grease into the river.

"It's going to be a big one," I say.

"How do you know?" he says.

"There's extra medicine in it," I say.

"Pardon?" he says.

"Never mind," I say.

"Tell you what," he says, "if it's still raining tomorrow morning early, I'll meet you at the Wavell outlet at 5:30 A.M."

I hang up and phone Dink. He says he'll be over at my place at five o'clock. I phone Connie Pan to see if she can come with us. I hear her ask her mother! Her mother's going to say, oh yes dear, you can go out at five o' clock in the morning with Bignose to look in a sewer!

Sure.

Connie Pan tells me she doesn't think she can go, but good luck.

I kill some time watching TV until around supper time. The storm is banging away outside, rattling the windows. I imagine everybody chasing their funny-looking vegetables and their fish down Somerset Street.

My mother isn't home from work. I slosh across the street through the storm to the Village Inn. She's over there sitting with some of her friends.

I sit in the empty chair beside her. Where my father used to sit. I can tell the way her friends are looking at me and at her that they've been talking about me, or she's been telling them about my job at the chipwagon and being unfired and probably about Dink and me, the private investigators. I get embarrassed when that happens. I know they do it because they're proud of you but you sometimes wish they wouldn't. Talk about you, I mean.

My mother tells me that she's been talking to Mrs. Pan and that they were talking about how her son was a friend of her daughter's and all that stuff. I tell her about tomorrow morning and the red dye, and what's going to happen at 5:30 A.M. if the storm keeps up. Then I tell her privately that I asked Connie to go but her mother won't let her.

"You'll have to get better acquainted with the Pan family before they're going to let her go out with the likes of you at five in the morning to look in a sewer!" my mother says.

This makes everybody smile. It's hard to have a private conversation with your mother in The Village Inn.

I tell her I'm going out for a while and I'll see her later. She says she'll be home a little later.

I go back home and dig around in the cupboard until I find my father's rain cape. I put it on, and his rain hat and go out into the storm on my bike. I go all the way out Richmond Road to Wavell. I cut across the Ottawa River Parkway to the outlet but it's dark and I can't make out anything.

But I can hear the water roaring in the pipe. I ride up Wavell, across on Tyndal, along Broadview, following the grease route. The streets are full of running water. I'm alone. Everybody is hiding inside behind their windows and doors. I can imagine the grease, flowing, red, under the wheels of my bike, in the tunnel below me.

I'm alone and I feel strong. Like I did on my ninth birthday by the small lake that time.

The storm sewers along the curb are sucking and gurgling like unplugged bathtubs. I ride all the way back to the Elmdale Tavern. My father's rain cape protects me from the thick driving rain. I stop at Dumper's truck and push a capsule into his barrel, right up to my shoulder. I race home, the rain pushing me from behind.

I grab some supper. While I'm washing up, my mother comes in and goes to bed. I bring her a hot chocolate.

"I'd like to go with you tomorrow if that's alright," she says.

I set the clock for 4:30 and go to bed.

Of course it's alright. That's the way it used to be. Do everything together.

It's hard to sleep and the storm outside is acting like it wants to come in and get into bed with me.

I dream a funny dream that makes me laugh. I don't know if I'm laughing in my dream or if I'm actually laughing in my bed. It's hard to tell. I know I'm dreaming but I can't wake up. My father and I are standing by Dumper's truck where he parks it and we are smiling. Dumper is under the truck dipping his hose in the storm sewer. My father raises his trombone. He blows a loud cavalry charge, only moving the slide slightly a couple of times. The notes are beautiful and clear and make your flesh bumpy. Dumper is so surprised he rises up under the truck and whacks his head and starts cursing. My father and I laugh.

Now, I'm dreaming I'm at the Wavell Avenue outlet. The music is frightening. It's some kind of Beethoven but it's played all wrong. I'm staring through the cage gate at the mouth of the pipe. Now the gate starts to push open. The bars of the gate are hung with filth. Floating towards me is something that is scaring me, making me sick with terror. It's a body. It's a person, floating, drowned in grease! The body floats closer. It floats on its stomach. Now it's stuck in the half-opened gate. It rolls over. I look at the face.

The face is my face!

My alarm rings.

I'm glad to get up and get rid of the dream.

My mother is up.

She will get the car out and follow a little later.

She knows where to go. On the Ottawa River Parkway, bottom of Wavell Avenue. She'll find it. She's got something to do first.

She's got a funny look on her face.

She's up to something, I can tell.

I make some peanut butter and toast and Dink shows up right on time and away we go to meet Eyebrows at the Wavell outlet. It's still raining but the storm is over. There's some blue showing in the early morning western sky. Eyebrows isn't there yet. The water is gushing out of the huge pipe into the Ottawa River. There's only one thing wrong. There's no red. What happened to the capsules? The red dye? I can't even tell if there's any grease in the water. There's so much gunk here. Mud, paper, gasoline, plastic, styrofoam, dog turds, cans, slime, dead fish . . .

A car pulls up and out gets Eyebrows. He looks happy and excited. He's so tall and with that big yellow rain slicker on, he looks like Big Bird.

"Well," he says, "what do you think?"

"Good storm," I say.

"Great storm!" he says.

"Where's the red river of rancid grease?" I say.

Eyebrows goes to his car and brings out a thing that looks like a small rocket launcher. But it's not a rocket launcher, it's a special light with different filters on it. He fiddles with the filters, then turns on the light, then adjusts the filters some more. He shines it on the opening of the pipe. Slowly, as he adjusts the filters, the liquid puking from the opening of the pipe through the gate turns pink, then bright red. He shines the light out into the water. A wide snake of red coils out into the Ottawa River.

Eyebrows lets out a victory shout.

"Well done, boys!" he shouts, while his eyebrows go nuts.

Another car pulls up and out gets guess who? My mother, Connie Pan and the driver, Mrs. Pan!

"Surprise!" says my mother, "look who I brought!"

Everybody's standing around smiling and talking and explaining and happy, just like we were getting ready to have a really great picnic.

My mother tells me all about how she left the Village Inn last night just after me and went over to the Pans' place, Mrs. Pan is her new friend from the Resource Centre, and she explained everything to Mrs. Pan about how I'm not really kicked out of school and how I'm working on this pollution case and everything. My mother's been helping Mrs.

Pan fill out the papers and get her driver's licence and buy this brand new used car she has.

Mrs. Pan is looking around, checking everything out.

She especially can't keep her eyes off Eyebrow's eyebrows!

Now he's on his cellular phone. Soon, a police car pulls up and two men get out. They have a little talk while Eyebrows lets me fool with the light while Dink shoots some pictures.

One is a picture of Connie and Mrs. Pan and me and my mother.

The red snake slides right out into the river and down towards Westboro Beach!

Good work, Nenaposh!

The cops get in their car.

Dink and I get in Eyebrow's car.

My mother and Connie get in Mrs. Pan's car.

The three cars speed over to Woodward Avenue where Dumper parks his truck. The truck is there. The barrel in the back is empty. The light shows the back of the truck red, the barrel red, the hose red, the pavement red, the sewer red.

We go over to Dumper's apartment building and find his apartment number on the mailboxes. We go up the stairs and the policeman in his uniform knocks on his door. The policeman in the grey suit has some papers and is writing notes.

In a while Dumper, half asleep, answers the door. He's holding up his pants with one hand. Eyebrows explains to him who we are and then the policeman with the grey suit reads from his paper all the stuff about Dumper and getting charged with polluting.

He starts off with, "Angelo Stubbs, I will point out to you your rights and I will then explain what you are being charged with."

While he's doing this, it takes Dumper a little while to catch on. As he is slowly understanding, Dink snaps his picture using the flash in the shadowy hallway of the apartment building.

All of a sudden, Dumper is awake.

Now he sees what's happening.

He remembers this flashing camera.

Now he stares at me.

He sees me now.

I look behind me. My mother is at the end of the hall, standing there. Behind her, peeking, is Connie Pan and her mom.

I look back at Dumper.

While the policeman is telling him when he's supposed to appear in court to answer these charges and while he's handing him the papers, Dumper is looking at me.

If these policemen weren't here right now, Dumper's eyes tell me, I would be dead.

Outside Dumper's apartment building everybody's thanking everybody and shaking hands.

I get in with Connie in the back seat of Mrs. Pan's new used car and my mother gets in the front. Mrs. Pan takes a last look at Eyebrows' eyebrows and gets in behind the wheel. She is sitting on a thick cushion.

Dink rides with the cops. We get dropped off at Westboro Beach and get our bikes.

We bike home.

I'm feeling pretty good.

In fact, I'm feeling very good.

There's no rain now and the sun is trying to come through the tame clouds. I change into my shirt with the silk buttercup pinned over the heart and go up to Somerset Street to work. Mr. Fryday is carefully parking his truck in front of the Mekong Grocery and, as usual, I remind him to switch off his parking lights. We get set up and he leaves.

About lunch time a man orders some chips and tells me he's a reporter from the *Ottawa Citizen* and can we talk about how the charges got laid against Mr. Stubbs and what part did I play. This reporter is a guy Eyebrows knows and it's pretty obvious Eyebrows already told him the whole thing. This reporter has already talked to Mr. Fryday so now *he* knows everything, too.

Then he tells me that I'm a hero and can he take my picture for tomorrow's paper. I don't mind at all. When the reporter's taking my picture, I'm standing in my chipwagon, I try to make my nose look as small as I can.

Then along comes Mr. Fryday and you can tell he's glad he's not involved in the crime but you can also tell he's worried about his brother-in-law and about how his poor wife will feel when she hears about it.

Then the reporter and Mr. Fryday have a chat and Mr. Fryday makes sure that the paper won't say anything bad about Fryday's Classical Chipwagons.

After the reporter leaves, Mr. Fryday thanks me for warning him about what Dumper was doing and tells me that I have actually saved his business and that he hopes that after I'm finished school I'll go in the chip business with him. I'll be his junior partner.

Then he tells me something that makes me feel empty.

"I'm terribly concerned about Angelo," he says. "I searched for him today after I found out what happened and I can't locate him anywhere. He was supposed to be doing trash at Rimsky-Korsakov's and also at Holtz's today but he never showed up. He has a terrible temper you know. This was always a great headache with us. If you trapped Angelo Stubbs in any way, he would often get very violent. Be careful of him, Spud Sweetgrass. Once, several years ago, a neighbour's dog barked at him one too many times. He did a terrible thing which brought the police. He seized the dog, a big Labrador it was, he grabbed it by the throat and lifted it off the ground and strangled it to death with his bare hands!"

Great!

XVI

I'm lying in a nice white bed in a hospital. There's the doctor. There's my mother. There's Connie Pan. And there's Dink the Thinker. And there's Mr. Fryday over there, his hands all bandaged. And there's the doctor telling us all about concussions. It's a jarring of the brain. No fractures, though. Be back to normal in two days. He means me. Be a bit scrambled for a while. Some memory loss. . . .

But wait a minute.

I remember some stuff, Mr. Doctor.

I remember reading the story in the paper. I was standing in the wagon, looking at the picture of myself in the paper and reading the headline: "YOUTHFUL SLEUTH NABS POLLUTER."

Then I read under the picture: "John 'Spud' Sweetgrass, hero."

I remember turning up Beethoven's Ninth Symphony, the Last Movement, the "Ode to Joy." And reading the part in the paper about Spud, the hero.

Then I remember Dink yelling, "Here comes Dumper in his truck!" I remember looking back down Somerset Street and seeing the truck coming, roaring up the hill and almost tipping over, two cop cars, chasing, swinging into the parking lane in front of Valentino's. But he wasn't parking. He was going at least twice the speed limit. He'll never get stopped behind me! Wait a minute. He's not trying to stop! He's picking up speed! He's flooring it! He's going to ram me!

I remember seeing his face through his windshield, Dumper's face, staring over the steering wheel, all red and squeezed up and insane. Dumper's truck coming so fast into the back of the chipwagon! He's trying to kill me!

And I remember diving out over the counter to get out of the wagon. I remember trying to dive carefully so I wouldn't knock over the salt and vinegar containers and the serviettes and make a mess. What a strange thing to be thinking at a time like that! And Beethoven's "Ode to Joy" blaring away!

Beethoven's "Ode to Joy," the happiest music Beethoven ever made.

But mostly, I remember Dumper's terrifying face.

And now I'm here in this white bed and Mr. Fryday is talking. While he is talking, saying thank God you're alright, I'm thinking, trying to think of something I forgot. Something I want to tell Mr. Fryday, something I used to tell him while we were getting the wagon ready. Oh yes! I know!

"Don't forget to turn off your parking lights, Mr. Fryday," I say.

I guess I just said something stupid because everybody has on a worried look now and my mother is squeezing my hand. But the doctor just laughs and tells everybody it's alright, it will all become clear in a very short time. Then I ask Mr. Fryday what happened to his hands, why are they all bandaged? Now Mr. Fryday starts crying. Now Dink shoves a picture in front of me. And he starts explaining.

It's a picture of somebody lying on the sidewalk on his face. His shirt is on fire. A man is beating out the flames with his bare hands. The man is Mr. Fryday. The person is me.

Dink shows me more pictures. And he's explaining. He sounds like a friend of my dad's who used to come over to our place and show us slides of his trips to the Northwest Territories.

He shows me a picture of the front of Dumper's truck, the big steel bumper crushing the back of the chipwagon, the propane tanks there. The front of Dumper's truck is a blur. One propane tank is halfway in the air, breaking apart over Dumper's hood. The other tank is bending in half, pushing into the wagon. The roof of the wagon is buckling. Dink says he's sorry that he didn't get the picture of the explosion because it happened right then, caused by an electrical spark because the tail lights were on. He says propane won't explode unless you give it an electric spark. So, if the parking lights were turned off, there wouldn't have been an explosion at all.

Is this why Mr. Fryday is crying?

The next picture is one of the guy who runs the Mekong Grocery. He's buried under a pile of boxes of noodles. Only his head is sticking out! He has a surprised look on his face.

In another picture, we see a fireman and a hose, hosing a burning truck and what's left of a chipwagon. In another picture, part of a sign with part of Beethoven's name on it, four wheels and a steering wheel and a policeman taking notes and almost everybody in Chinatown standing around. I make a joke. "I guess the fries were overdone this time, eh, Mr. Fryday?" Mr. Fryday starts crying all over again.

In another picture there's an ambulance and a stretcher and the stretcher being lifted up and me, on the stretcher, laughing and waving at the camera!

"You were acting very strange after you hit your head and after Mr. Fryday put out your burning shirt. It's the concussion. You're still acting a little weird, if you want to know the truth!" says Dink.

Now, Dink has today's *Ottawa Sun* with him. He shows me the front page. The whole front page is a big colour photograph of the crowd in Chinatown watching the chipwagon and the truck burn down. Lots of people we know are in the picture. Right in the centre there's a group. Like a wedding picture. In the group I can see two or three waiters from Valentino's. Also in the group I see six or seven half-naked women in high heels. And, right in the middle of the group, the star of the group: Guess who?

That's right.

Mr. Boyle, hot-shot teacher!

Dink draws a circle around Mr. Boyle with a ball point.

"Guess where this picture's going to hang pretty soon?" says Dink.

"Where?" I say, feeling too tired to guess.

"Inside your locker door at Tech when you go back," says Dink.

Then Dink shows me one last photograph, by Dink, master photographer.

A photograph of a man with high pants, running up Somerset Street.

I look at Dink.

He nods.

It's Dumper, alright.

Dumper, on the run!

"Listen to this," says Dink. "Here's what Dumper's charged with." Dink reads from a list: "dangerous driving, careless driving, speeding, impaired driving, criminal negligence, property damage, assault, resisting an officer, hit and run, public mischief, forgery, failing to stop at five intersections, operating a vehicle without a licence, leaving the scene, fraud and illegal dumping of toxic substances!"

"They forgot one," I say.

"Which one is that?" asks Mr. Fryday, blowing his nose.

"Insulting a person's father," I say.

Now the nurse comes in the room and kicks everybody out. My mother promises she'll be back to see me as soon as she gets off work. She gives me a big wink and lets go my hand.

The last person to leave is Connie Pan.

She leans over the bed and kisses me on the forehead. It feels nice. She takes my hand. Her face looks like it's in technicolour. It must be because of my concussion.

No! It's not the concussion!

She's wearing lipstick!

Yecch!

Should I tell her about where lipstick comes from?

No, I better not. I don't want to hurt her feelings.

When she leaves, I'll have a sleep.

I'm pretty tired. And my back stings a bit.

Maybe, after I'm asleep the nurse will come in and give my forehead a wipe for me. Rub the red grease off.

Connie Pan leaves.

I'll go to sleep now.

I hope I'll dream.

Too bad you can't pick your dreams. If you could, I would pick my favourite dream, the one of my father playing "Hanging Gardens" on his trombone.

That would be nice.

❧

Epilogue

I can smell cooking trout on a stick over a fire. I can feel my dad's and my mom's arms around me that morning after breakfast . . . I feel their tears of joy on my cheeks. Victory! I made it! I made it alone!

FRY-DAY